DEMETRIUS

SINGLE DADS OF GAYNOR BEACH

SA SWAY & SKYLER DRAKE

Demetrius
(Single Dads of Gaynor Beach)
© 2022 SA Sway & Skyler Drake

ISBN-13: 978-1-990307-22-5 (ebook)
ISBN-13: 978-1-990307-32-4 (paperback)

Published by Blue Crescent Books
Edited by Ashley Rayner at Inkwell's Editorial
Cover Design and Formatting by Irish Ink Publishing

First Edition: October 11, 2022
10 9 8 7 6 5 4 3 2 1

ABOUT DEMETRIUS
(SINGLE DADS OF GAYNOR BEACH)

Hotshot architect Demetrius Johnson is too young to be starting over after divorcing his childhood sweetheart. But when you're a dad, you learn to put your responsibilities first and your feelings last.

That's why he moved to Gaynor Beach in Southern California for a new job to support his son and start over. But, unfortunately, it's also why he has to put up with Miguel.

Miguel is everything Demetrius isn't—reckless, careless, playful, and spontaneous. But, most of all, he's dangerous because he's making Demetrius feel something he's never felt before.

Straight out of his only long-term relationship, with a ten-year-old struggling to adjust, Demetrius knows he's too old to question his sexuality. But he can't help his growing attraction to his flirtatious new co-worker.

Will Miguel find a way to show Demetrius that he's more than a good time? Or will the pressure be too much for this young single father trying to rebuild his life?

Demetrius **is a gay single dad contemporary romance set in the shared world of Gaynor Beach, featuring an age-gap, interracial, opposites-attract love story where both partners share more than a few first times, raising a precocious tween ready to cause chaos along the way.**

CHAPTER 1

DEMETRIUS

NOTHING SCREAMS NEW BEGINNINGS LIKE TOTALING YOUR CAR ON the run from your past.

With a groan, I cracked my back and resisted the urge to kick my blown-out tire. Scuffing my new leather shoes would only add to my bad mood, and I wasn't going to have money to spare before I got my next paycheck.

Wiping at my sweaty face, I couldn't help but wonder how long it would be until a tow truck arrived. My son and I needed to get off this highway median before we melted or got hit by another car.

The sun was already beating down on my back, and Lord knew I had never been a good mechanic, barely knowing my way around a flat.

Buildings, I understood. Monuments too. Restoration architecture had been my bread and butter for five years, and I was damn good at it.

So you'd think maintaining and preserving a machine wouldn't be much different, right?

Wrong.

I paid people to do that for me.

1

Past popping a hood, or anything beyond replacing a flat tire, I was like an infant being taught advanced trigonometry.

I was *way* over my head.

Or in deep shit, as my mom loved to say.

And speaking of parents, I could practically hear my dad in my ear chewing me out, accusing me of being a fuck up for not being able to do something "all men should be able to do."

Though, I guessed my situation was outside the scope of most men, as my front bumper was hanging on for dear life. A wheel on the front and one on the rear were blown. And bits of glass and chunks of metals were strewn across the median.

I was no expert, but I'd be surprised if my car could be fixed at all.

"Fuck," I gritted out, dazed and confused and at a loss for words.

I was going to make myself dizzy pacing around, hoping every loud honking horn or heavy thud was Golden Bear Towing flying down I-805 to rescue us from this California heat, ferrying us to Norton Automotive.

But, alas, I was stuck on that highway to hell.

"Dad!" I looked up and over at a rolled-down window. "It's Mom. She said, *'answer your phone, now!'* Grandma called her. I told you she would."

I sighed, avoiding eye contact with my ten-year-old son, who did the same. He was doing his best stank face in the back of the car, listening to some obscure rapper that made my ears bleed since the volume was on "way too fucking loud."

Meech's headphones were practically rammed down his ears, and I was sure he wouldn't hear me respond even if I attempted to.

So I didn't. And I didn't tell him to turn it down either. What was the point when I personally would've loved to be

drowning everything out? I couldn't blame him for his atti-
tude back then.

It wasn't like I could've anticipated a mattress flying off
the back of a pickup truck. But even so, I wasn't happy about
nearly killing us both trying to avoid it.

People tended to complain I was a perfectionist, and I
used to brush the critique off. But I'd never felt more off-kilter
in my life, and I couldn't find a way to cope.

Nothing made sense. Nothing was going as planned. And
I didn't know what to do next.

Besides calling back my son's mother, who probably
almost had a heart attack at the news. It was bad enough that
my mama treated my ex like her real daughter and told her
what happened behind my back before I got a chance to
compose myself.

Now I knew they'd be up late gossiping about how I
should've stayed in Maryland instead of attempting this
cross-country journey by car, alone, and how I should've just
flown us here if I saw no other way to start over.

If only shipping wasn't so outrageous, I would've. Or, in
the words of my mama, if I wasn't so damn cheap.
Bless her.

Filling my car to the max helped offset the cost of the
move, until this unfortunate sequence of events. And now I'd
worn myself out driving for nothing, really.

Digging in my back pocket, I whipped out my phone and
swallowed my pride. Sure enough, there were three missed
calls plus five messages from my "WIFE."

And the three dots aggressively blinking at me warned me
she was about to fire off a few more.

"Shit...," I muttered under my breath, wedging the phone
between my ear and shoulder as I looked for the tow truck.
"Hello? Hello~ Oh, good. Denise, look—"

She picked up and cut me off right away.

"Thank God you're both okay! What the hell happened,

Tri? Meechie said something about a mattress!? Are you hurt?"

Some tension rolled away, replaced with anxiety, as I tried to calm her down and walk her through what happened.

Denise sounded so afraid. And that was normal. Her son wasn't picking up, and though I was her *ex*-husband, it wasn't like all our feelings for each other had disappeared overnight after we divorced. Even if they weren't romantic anymore, we still cared deeply for each other.

Hell, it had only been three months since we made things official, even though it already felt like it had been three years.

Which reminded me that I really needed to change her contact on my phone.

But that was beside the point. It was normal for a mother to be so fearful after an accident. I would've been the same way. I *was* the same way, an emotional wreck.

Despite those obvious facts, it just drove home the fact that I'd lost control of my life. Denise and my son made me feel more like a fucking loser with each passing day. And for the first time in a long time, I agreed with that assessment.

First a marriage in shambles, then a son closing himself off from me brick by emotional brick. And now a pile of junk that used to be a car to top off this shitstorm.

I dreaded thinking about what was waiting for me next in this cosmic game of "fuck Demetrius Johnson, Jr." that had been going on for a little over a year.

With a heavy sigh, I murmured, "Talk soon, okay? Once we're in town, I'll call you back for sure."

"Okay," Denise said, a small tremor in her voice. "Call me when you can. Stay safe…"

There was an awkward silence where "I love you" would usually come as naturally as breathing between us.

"Love you." I worked up the courage to say it first

because I would've thrown myself into oncoming traffic if the awkward pause went on any longer.

I just couldn't handle awkwardness anymore. I was over it, truly.

"... Love you too! I'm so sorry, Tri. I hope everything goes well with work tomorrow. If you can't make it, don't worry about it. Though, I guess you're still planning to go in either way... But I'm sure the company will understand if you let them know what happened."

I chewed my bottom lip.

Am I that much of a workaholic that she just assumes I'd roll into work after all this? Ding, ding. Of course I am. She knows me best.

"Of course, of course. Bye."

"Bye-bye. And tell Meechie to answer *his* phone too."

I hung up after nodding as if she could see me. If there was one thing Denise was anal about, it was picking up your phone when she called. Where my anxieties manifested into overthinking, hers always took the form of us getting killed or kidnapped when we let something go to voicemail too many times.

I blamed True Crime; those serial killer shows and podcasts had you thinking everyone was out to get out.

"Dad?" Meechie called out, and for once, his bright white AirPods weren't drilled into his ears.

You'd think he was recently going through puberty with the 180-degree turn in his personality.

"Hm?" I asked as I came up beside the window, taking off my glasses to wipe them down.

"Are we going to be okay?"

Damn it. It was a simple question, and yet again, I was at a loss for words.

We were going to be okay in the short term, at least. I had enough saved up for this to be a major inconvenience, but nothing more until the insurance check came. A moving pod was still hauling our life down to Southern California, as I had enough insight not to try to tow it myself beforehand.

But his question conjured up visions of the future that were murky at best when it all used to be so crystal clear.

Are we going to be okay? I have no fucking clue!

"Yes," I said with confidence I didn't really have. "We'll be fine. And once that truck comes, we'll crash at a hotel tonight since most of our stuff is probably damaged. Then we'll be in our new home when the pod arrives. You and me. Together."

He nodded, a peculiar twinkle in his dark brown eyes, and seemed to relax from that tiny reassurance. He went back to scrolling on his phone, cool as could be. Though, he was still ignoring Denise's messages.

And I knew he wasn't faking it, how relaxed Meechie was. I could always tell when he was really antsy or nervous. His emotions, unlike mine, always appeared on his face.

Demetrius Johnson, III might be his government name, but he acted nothing like me and absolutely didn't resemble his grandpa. He was too collected to be only ten and most definitely didn't share the family trait—being anal about everything and anything 24/7.

I tapped the hood of the car and turned around, leaning against the frame. The sun was still beaming down, but I was feeling a bit more hopeful then.

Though I wished Denise was there to be the intermediary. She was always better with words. But that wasn't an option anymore.

I showed love by doing and providing. And I couldn't provide much of anything for Meechie until this *goddamned* tow truck showed up.

You're young; you'll find love again…

I'm so sorry…

Could be worse; at least it's amicable…

None of my friends' and family's platitudes really helped

in the wake of those simple words, "I want a divorce," that changed my life forever.

I was way too young to be starting all over, uprooting, and moving halfway across the country on top of it all.

But all I could do was hope to mend my broken heart in a new town and repair my relationship with my son, seeing as he was all I really had left now.

Oh, and fix my front bumper, if possible. That would be great!

CHAPTER 2

MIGUEL

I CLIMBED DOWN THE SCAFFOLDING WITH A REGRETFUL SMILE already pulling at my lips.

Dan was at the bottom waiting, not looking so happy. Instead of saying anything when I hopped down, he shrugged sadly, but I wasn't really the type to let goodbyes get the better of me.

"You're done already?" I demanded, slapping his arm playfully. "Who is going to install that floor now?"

He grinned.

"That's on you now, buddy. Like it was supposed to be from the start."

I shook my head, forever teasing that Dan had to man up and help with the labor despite being the project manager. Well, former project manager now.

"No way. My old knees can barely bend anymore, and you expect me to kneel on them?"

"Always complaining," Chris said, climbing down behind me and passing me to give Dan a hug and a pat on the back.

"It's been great working with you," Chris said. "Best project manager I ever had."

"We love you, Dan!" Mike shouted from above. "It won't be the same here without you!"

Dan laughed.

"Okay, you guys can stop bullshitting me now."

"It's true," I argued. "Who else is going to let us drink beers onsite?"

"Sh," Dan hushed, glancing around. "Don't mention that to anyone, yeah?"

Chris chuckled.

"Come on, the end of the day on a Friday doesn't count. No one would mind."

Dan shook his head. "I don't know. I heard my replacement is a real stickler for details."

"Shit, really? He a hard ass?" Chris asked, instantly looking worried.

Chris was the sensitive type. He couldn't help but worry and overthink unless you distracted him. I waved his concern away, stopping the turn in the conversation.

"He'll be fine," I insisted with a cheeky smile. "Who could resist being friends with us?"

Chris sighed, but Dan laughed along.

"True. You're all irresistible. I'm going to miss you three."

Dan was more than a work colleague. After more than two years with Smithson Construction, our little team had become close friends. I didn't know many other people in Gaynor Beach. I didn't need to. On weekdays we worked together; on weekends, we often met up socially. Mike was a fishing aficionado, and I went out with him on his boat more weekends than not. Other times, Chris and I went rock climbing, or Dan invited us all out to his place for barbeques with his family. Those were my favorite days, when the hours stretched on, the sun shone down on us, the air smelled like smoked sausages, and the kids climbed all over me until I threw them into the pool and jumped in after them.

It really wouldn't be the same without Dan around.

But with two kids, another on the way, and no relatives in town, Dan and his wife had decided to move closer to their families in San Jose.

That meant one of my closest friends would be hours away and we would be getting a new project manager starting tomorrow.

But right now, Dan was still here.

"Enough of all this crying," I said, hooking an arm around his shoulders and steering him away from Chris, who seemed to be on a downward spiral.

"What are we doing now?" I asked.

Dan looked at me, an amused smile tilting his lips as if he knew what was coming.

"Now?" he demanded. "I promised Lea I'd be home to help with the packing."

"She won't mind," I insisted.

"What's Miguel trying to convince you to do now?" Chris asked, following after us.

I grinned at him over my shoulder.

"Just a couple beers at The Cantina."

Finally descending the scaffold, Mike fist-pumped the air.

"Yes! It's a beautiful day. I could use a beer."

I looked at Chris, who sighed and nodded.

"It would be nice to down a couple before you're off."

Dan groaned, even though I knew he was always up for hanging out with his friends.

"Okay, okay, just let me call Lea."

Lea, as always, let Dan get away with it. According to him, she "knew what we were like" which, I assumed, was not meant in an insulting way since she always greeted us each with a big hug.

Either way, we ended up in The Gaynor Cantina, still in our work clothes, coated in sawdust.

The moment we walked in, Evan, the slim blond who was the head bartender, grinned and waved.

He was helping someone else, so we settled on the barstools by the open front wall.

"His name's Demetrius," Dan was saying to Chris. "I spoke to him on the phone, walked him through some of the issues we were having, like the buckled wall."

I thought I could guess who they were talking about.

"Your replacement?" I asked, to be sure.

Dan nodded.

"He should be all up to speed for tomorrow. He was sent the updated plans. You might have to help him out a bit at first. It's hard to switch PM halfway through a project."

I shrugged.

"He'll do fine. We'll help him."

Suddenly, a large glass of my favorite lager slid in front of me.

Evan caught my eye with his usual smirk, sliding the boys each their favorite drink.

"Wow, we didn't even have to order," Dan said. "You'd think we've been here before."

"I must be psychic," Evan agreed and crossed his arms, leaning against the bar. "What are you lads up to tonight?"

"I'm moving," Dan said. "Today was my last day at work with these guys."

"Oh shit."

Immediately, Evan pulled out shot glasses.

"How many?" he wondered. "Ten? Will ten do?"

I laughed while Dan and Chris groaned.

"Not tequila, at least," Dan begged as the tequila was poured.

Mike was howling with laughter.

"Oh buddy," he said to Evan. "Big mistake. You do not want to see that guy on tequila."

He pointed at me and I grinned.

Truthfully, the last time the tequila had been brought out, I

11

couldn't quite remember what I had been like, but it didn't matter.

The sun was shining, I was with my friends, and I had a drink in my hand. Life couldn't get any better.

Without hesitating, I threw back my shot, following with the lime and a wink.

"As long as I'm home by six," Dan said, tipping his shot into his mouth and promptly choking.

Considering that later that night, at some godawful hour, I stumbled up the sidewalk towards my small, bright blue rental house in Oakdale, it was safe to say that *none* of us were home by six.

At least Dan wouldn't have to work in the morning.

Groaning, I climbed up the front steps. My stomach started gurgling by the time I reached my door. The house was quaint, maybe even a little shabby, but it was right by the beach. The large houses on the other side took the view, but I was still by the fresh air and a short walk would take me to the ledges on the other side where I could take it all in. All I ever needed was that big sky and the ocean below it.

Without turning on the lights, somehow, despite all laws of the universe, I made it into bed without puking and shut my eyes in the dark while the room swayed and spun around me.

As a wild young thing, I had lamented growing older. I'd thought life would have to slow down and I didn't want that. Yet here I was, turning forty soon and still partying when the opportunity arose.

Of course, my recovery was not what it used to be, and back then, I'd always had someone by my side to hold my hair back so to speak. Maria first, then Rodrigo for what I had thought would be forever.

My two big relationships had each held their own problems. Maria, my first love, back home in Argentina, had been so driven that it was scary and oppressive. She wanted money and land, and I wanted to have fun and travel.

The opportunity to come to America to live with a distant aunt had ended us but introduced me to Rodrigo a couple years later. We'd had so much in common that it was doomed to crash and burn from the start. When you had two people searching for adventure, they were bound to find it elsewhere. Rodrigo had, anyway, with some hot guy at the gym he frequented.

That type of hurt was best avoided, I reminded myself and stretched out my arms, feeling the empty bed around me.

At least now I had room and all the covers to myself.

I laughed suddenly in the silence and then had to stop and breathe before my stomach upended itself.

When the wave of nausea subsided, I glanced over at my digital clock and sighed. It was nearly three AM. Work started at seven-thirty. That gave me and the boys only four hours to sleep and sober up... and on the day our new project manager was starting.

That poor bastard. Demetrius, was it? Hopefully, he showed up on his first day with coffees and a good sense of humor. We would all need it.

CHAPTER 3
DEMETRIUS

IF IT WASN'T ONE DISASTER, IT WAS ANOTHER WAITING AROUND the corner for me as of late. As much as I hated having a constant pity party in my head, life seemed to be a train wreck lately. Or a car wreck, to be more exact.

"Stop right here. Yes, yes. Thank you," I said, dragging my things out of my rideshare as we pulled up at 642 Winchelsea Road in the Willis Cove neighborhood.

I arrived a few minutes late on my first day at work. Untypical for me, but what could I do? Between having to get Meechie up, ready, and fed solo for the first time in ten years, then having to wait on my ride to pick me up, it was a wonder I didn't miss my first day altogether.

On top of that, as we drove by what could only be described as a giant country club, my ride and I got stopped in front of this gated community. A fact that the owner of the property I'd be working on failed to mention. Or remember, seeing as he was heading into early retirement for a reason.

A few desperate phone calls later, the gatekeeper finally let us in.

"Thanks," I called over my shoulder, leaving a tip on the app as my ride drove away.

Taking in a deep breath, I glanced at the rows of trees decked out in autumn yellows and oranges. The streets were silent thanks to it being back-to-school week. Only a few people mingled around on porches, what I assumed was hired help doing landscaping.

Quiet suburbia. Or, more accurately, quiet HOA-enforced luxury with a suburban veneer. One look at these million-dollar homes, and the pointed stares from some people walking by, told me all I needed to know about who lived in Willis Cove.

It was vastly different from the area my son and I were staying in, as I got a mortgage on an older home until I could get back on my feet. Alimony wasn't cheap, and until Denise was able to sell our old home, I didn't want to get into anything too expensive alone.

"Let's do this."

The imposing Japanese-style house I walked up to stood out starkly from the hyper-modern buildings lining the rest of the road.

Fumbling with my tie, and adjusting my glasses, I entered Smithson Construction's work site with my back against the door. I tried to balance my briefcase in one hand with an arm full of schematic designs for this historical property in the other.

Winchelsea House would be a challenge to repair between the maze of construction codes and the need for specific building materials in the middle of a supply chain nightmare. Historic homes always put up more than a few barriers in the best of conditions. But I was up to the challenge. I had to be.

I was anal about work to begin with, but this gig was even more demanding. My former architectural design professor, Mr. Hiroshi Furukawa, was the only reason I was able to pick up and move cross country in the first place. He'd recommended me to Smithson Construction after the PM left, and there were fears the project would be put on hold. I had jumped at the chance. It paid well, well enough to leave Bethesda behind. And the business owners worked outside of the country, in Canada or something, so they were used to running the business through competent PMs.

I needed a reason to leave, and Mr. Furukawa offered it in the form of a well-paying restoration of his family's estate. Well, at first. Then it became a demanding remodel for him to move into with his very pregnant daughter, with issues like a buckled wall and a mountain of permits to get through. I had to check the brief again to be sure, but the former project manager, Dan, had given me the rundown of the ups and downs of this particular project.

Which meant I needed my team to stay focused, get shit done, and preferably stay under budget.

Failure was not an option.

However, as I scaled the steps to the second floor, the bottom floor already in demolition, I didn't see anyone that looked like they were the foreman to help me kickstart the process.

"Hey, how are you? Are you new around here?" I stopped in my tracks as a smooth, accented voice greeted me.

I craned my head to the side and found a man casually sipping on a thermos full of coffee, if the smell was any indication. He was tall, only an inch or two shorter than me, and I was six two.

The stranger swooped his black hair back, dark stubble covering his angular chin. He had standard construction gear on: brown steel-toed boots, khaki-colored work pants that hung loosely around his legs with a plethora of pockets and built in kneepads, and a form-fitting white tank top covered in sawdust and some dirt.

He looked like a laborer, lean with muscle. Rugged, even. His olive-brown skin and broad shoulders made him appear younger. But, on closer inspection, he was definitely older than me, with a casual air about him full of charm. Especially his eyes. It felt like he was piercing my soul, the vibrant green a little unnerving. Curiosity sparked in those depths, along with something I couldn't quite place.

I didn't know how to address him. The more I stared at him, I couldn't quite peg his age. Maybe late thirties or early forties, though he could pass for his late twenties.

I forced a smile, finally settling on, "Hello. Yes, I am."

I wanted to keep things short. Not that I was trying to be an asshole, but I was already too overwhelmed as it stood. I just wanted to speak to the new foreman, get started on our plans, and then retreat into my soon-to-be studio to go over the architect's designs.

Manage the project and not get too caught up in the day-to-day. That was my ideal scenario going forward. Me and the crew could bond later.

But this stranger wasn't having it as he cozied up next to me. Too close, actually, forcing me to step away as he continued to sip on his coffee.

"Name's Miguel. It's nice to meet you. We don't get too many new guys around here. Don't remember Dan saying anything about a new worker. Where are you from? I was born in Argentina, but when I got an opportunity to go to trade school up north, I took it. I moved here a few years ago. Never looked back. Hmm, what else? Oh! Yes, I've been working at Smithson as the head carpenter for about… five or six years. Give or take. Great crew, you'll love them. This is my second time restoring a house out in Willis Cove. A lot of deep pockets out here…"

Miguel didn't give me time to get a word in as he started rambling on and on about this and that. Every so often, I tried to interject, but he just kept talking, and I didn't have the energy to stop him.

"What's your name?" Finally, a question for me.

"Demetrius. It's nice to meet you." I scanned the floor for more men, but it just seemed to be us. Which was odd.

His eyes widened, like something clicked.

"Ah, so it's you. Demetrius. Hm... How old are you? Where are you from, again? You don't sound like you're from here. East coast, maybe?"

Now I was getting annoyed. It wasn't like I didn't want to get to know the guys, but maybe later at night while watching a game. Not at 7:35 in the morning when I hadn't had so much as a piece of toast.

"I'm really sorry, ah—"

"Miguel," he said, flashing rows of pearly white teeth, aside from what looked like a piece of lettuce stuck between his front teeth. "It's nice to meet the new PM."

"Miguel," I echoed with a genuine smile, trying to keep myself from laughing at him as I tapped my lips. But he didn't seem to pick up on my silent cue.

He cocked his head to the side, reminding me of a puppy, which was strange. He was a grown-ass man, but it was sort of... cute. In a disgusting way.

"You have something in your teeth," I murmured, looking away as he sucked them, trying to get the food bits out.

"Thanks!"

"No problem. I'd love to chat some more, but I need to meet with the foreman to finalize our plan of action. Maybe we can catch up—" Again, I was interrupted.

He tapped his chest lightly, downing the rest of his coffee before saying, "That would be me. I'm the foreman."

Blinking rapidly, I knew my jaw would be on the damn floor if it wasn't buried behind rolls of paper. I didn't need to check my watch to know we had probably wasted ten minutes chatting about nonsense, wasting precious time we should have been working.

"And you're the new project manager. So I'm glad we could meet first thing."

It took everything in me not to roll my eyes at that.

"Who else would I be? Aren't you expecting me?"

And didn't he just say they don't see too many new faces around here?

"I thought you just wandered in here, one of those architectural interns or something Dan forgot to tell me about, you know? But then I remembered Dan said the new PM's name was Demetrius, and it clicked."

"Do I look like an intern to you?"

Who the hell expects strangers to walk onto a construction site unsupervised? In this community, of all places?

I was beginning to suspect Miguel was a bit of an airhead.

He looked me up and down. I shifted uncomfortably under his steady gaze.

"I mean... you do look pretty young. Too young to be a project manager, at the very least."

This time I couldn't suppress my shock, huffing. And I knew very well I was sneering too.

"I assure you I have enough experience."

He went from an inconvenience to an annoyance quickly. And I wasn't in the mood to deal with him.

We had been in each other's presence for less than an hour, and he was already questioning my ability to get the job done. Things weren't getting off to a good start.

He backtracked, shaking his hands in front of my face, "No! That's not what I meant. I mean—"

"Forget it. I'm going to set up my office. We need to talk."

Holding my chin up just a bit, I started walking towards what I hoped was an empty room. I stopped by the door when I realized I didn't have any way to get inside without dropping half of my shit on the ground.

With a sigh, I spun around and marched back, nudging my head towards my door. "A little help would go a long way. My arms are pretty full."

He smirked. A shit-eating grin, really.

"Of course."

I wondered vaguely if it was possible to beg my parents to

stay with them a few more months, and walk back to Maryland on foot rather than spend another waking moment with this man. And we still had a few months ahead of us for this project.

Fuck me.

CHAPTER 4

MIGUEL

I FINALLY FORCED MYSELF OUT OF BED TWENTY MINUTES LATER than usual. I was a morning person naturally and didn't like to stick around the house too much. Normally, I was bouncing out the door with a coffee in my thermos and a bagel in my hand an hour before I had to leave.

I sometimes liked to catch the tail end of the sunrise lifting over the ocean sitting on the bench at the Gaynor Beach Pier. There was no better way to start the day.

Today, though, I found my feet dragging.

I took too long in the shower and made myself a proper breakfast of eggs and toast. By the time I was dressed in my work gear and ready to go, I would have to pray for no traffic to even make it on time.

The gods didn't listen. Or maybe they did, because there was construction en route and I was glad.

Normally, work was my getaway. I saw my friends, worked with my hands, and completed rewarding projects.

That was before *Demetrius* though.

The man was such a wet blanket that it was turning into a headache just seeing him.

Sitting in traffic, I sipped my coffee and realized that the morning sunlight was still sending gold streaks through the sky.

With a pleased sigh, I sat back, relaxing as I waited. I would get there when I got there, and I would force Demetrius to relax somehow.

For a week now, he had been terse and stiff. The man didn't seem to have any sense of humor whatsoever. I had tried multiple times to joke with him while we went over plans for the day and was rewarded with not so much as a smile. He ate lunches alone in the office space he'd claimed, and he practically ran from the house at the end of the day.

And he seemed so young. I guessed he was still in his twenties. At that age, I'd been backpacking through Asia without a penny in my pocket. I'd partied with people I didn't know. I'd *lived.* I sure as hell hadn't been a supervisor on an expensive contract, and I hadn't spent years in school for an architectural degree or any degree for that matter.

It was hard for me to imagine a life so full of deadlines and pressure that a young man couldn't even smile.

As I pulled into a parking spot in the gated community where we were working, just across the street from the house we were working on, I realized I didn't think I'd ever known anyone like him.

It was with that thought that I hopped out of my truck and climbed the front steps.

Inside, the guys were unpacking their gear in the main room, which had already been stripped down to studs.

"We thought you got in an accident," Mike said. "No one was whistling or singing when we arrived."

"It was eerie," Chris agreed, grinning.

I shrugged.

"I slept in boys, it happens to the best of us."

Demetrius strode in then, face set in that serious way, dark

22

eyes focused behind his glasses. He opened his mouth to speak, but I went on before he could.

"Not to this guy though," I said. "Demetrius is a machine. You would never miss a day of work, not even if your house was on fire, right?"

His stride faltered, full lips parting in surprise for a moment before his features smoothed again.

"Why do you say that?" he asked, voice guarded.

I shrugged, curiosity rising at his reaction.

"You seem like a serious guy." I winked. "All work and no play."

He looked away, swallowed, and when he turned back, I knew my remarks hadn't landed well.

Again, that serious, almost blank expression…

"We have to get started on the staircase addition today," he said.

"But we didn't finish framing in the new wall."

"I know, and the drywall crew will be in on Wednesday. Can we split you guys up?"

"I'll start the stairs, you two finish the wall," I said to the boys.

I looked at Demetrius for approval and he nodded slightly before turning and walking away.

The man was a mystery.

Shaking my head, I went to what had been the kitchen, looking at the smooth cement floor for a moment. Century homes like these were harder to work on, since they required more permits, inspections, and special materials. Somehow, we'd gotten the go-ahead to cut a new staircase in.

Before I could pull up the plans on my phone, Demetrius was suddenly at my side again, holding open the large printed sheets of paper.

I helped him pull the extra sheets aside until we reached the plans for this room, but my attention was drawn away from the light blue lines and measurements to the man standing next to me.

We hadn't gotten so close to each other yet and the clean, masculine scent of whatever soap and aftershave he used filled my senses.

I found myself leaning slightly closer despite myself. Demetrius didn't notice; he was tilting his head at the plans, all his focus glued to the pages.

"So, it's going to be placed here," he said. "We need two landings on the way down, every four steps."

I found myself smiling.

"First, I have to cut the hole," I said.

He nodded.

"Right, of course."

"What do you do for fun?" I suddenly found myself asking.

"Fun?" He stared at me for a moment and then finally seemed to notice how close I was and took a step back.

"Um..."

I chuckled.

"If you need to think that hard, then you need to get out more. Come on, are you free tonight?"

He looked completely taken aback and, for a moment, I thought I pushed too far, but he simply shook his head.

Part of me wanted to insist, but somehow, I managed to keep my lips sealed.

"Alright, well, if you want to go for drinks with me and the guys anytime, you're welcome."

He handed me the plans and nodded curtly.

"I don't like drinking," he said. "Especially not on a Monday."

And with that, he left.

I could have kicked myself.

The guy couldn't stand me... but being me, that only made

me want to win him over even more. The fact that he smelled as good as he looked didn't hurt either.

Surprised at the turn of my thoughts, I shook my head and laid the plans out on the counter, bending over them.

It was hard to concentrate though.

Demetrius *was* fine as hell. He had that solid dark complexion, a strong jaw, and those *lips*. He was masculine and soft at the same time. He looked like the type of guy I would love to hold under a blanket on a cold night and make love to until morning.

He was so moody though. And undoubtedly straight. And we worked together. Oh, and he hated me.

I snorted.

It would still be best to make friends somehow. I loved my job and I had never loved a job enough to want to stick around for it before. The idea of it getting tarnished because of one sour co-worker made a strange, lost feeling fill my chest.

Why did Dan have to leave like that? Dammit, I already missed him and his family so much.

I didn't have one of my own. Having him and Mike and Chris had made me feel less like I was lacking something.

The Autumn Festival started this weekend. It wouldn't be the same without his kids, Perry and Lexi. Who was I going to take on all the rides? I didn't think Chris or Mike would be down for apple bobbing and pumpkin picking with me. They'd do the Oktoberfest pub crawl at the very least, but that wasn't the best part of autumn in Gaynor Beach, in my opinion. This town really was made for families.

I swallowed and finally managed to squash my wandering thoughts.

I focused on the task at hand, even finding some joy in it. For break time, I only took the time to microwave my coffee and take a couple of sips before getting back into it. By the time lunch came around, I was feeling more like myself again.

Keeping busy, working hard, and concentrating while building up a sweat always positively affected me.

I was starving by lunch, but before making my usual trip a couple blocks over to pick up a sub, I noticed that Demetrius was nowhere to be seen. Probably still holed up in his office.

Maybe he needed to be reminded to eat. He did seem like that type.

I climbed the steps, pausing outside the door at the resonant sound of his voice, which carried like a soft rumble. It was slightly ajar, just enough that I could see his shape pacing anxiously into view and then out again.

"You're joking. Can anything be done for it?"

Silence rang, and a moment later, a soft sigh.

"Sure. I'll get a ride in after work to talk about it."

Judging by the heavy sigh that turned into a groan midway through, I assumed he hung up the call.

I bit my lip, wondering if I should back away, pretend I hadn't been standing outside the door listening.

Instead, I knocked softly, allowing the door to drift open as I did, exposing Demetrius bent over his desk with his elbows braced on the surface, his face in his hands.

He looked up at me, face slack with surprise for a moment, and I smiled and shrugged.

"I was just coming to remind you that it's lunchtime."

He stared at me for what felt like a full minute.

"I know it's lunchtime," he finally said.

"Right, well... you need a ride?"

The words just slid out of my mouth, and as soon as they were out, I knew I wasn't going to rest until he agreed.

"You don't have a car anymore, right? What happened to it?"

When his expression hardened, I held up my hands innocently.

"I'll take you to the mechanic," I said, "after work."

"I'm good. Thanks."

"You don't sound good."

His jaw visibly clenched, but I ignored it, trying my hardest to melt him with a friendly smile.

"Look, you're my new co-worker. I couldn't rest letting you cab, or take a bus when I have a truck right outside the door. We'll leave right at 3:30."

His jaw dropped, but I winked and swiftly took off down the stairs before he could argue any further.

CHAPTER 5

DEMETRIUS

I'll pick you up at 3:30. Point, blank, period. Miguel didn't give me a chance to respond before his head disappeared behind the closed door, leaving me stunned and amazed.

My co-worker was truly an enigma to me. One moment he seemed like he wanted to be my best friend, and the next, he was making some snide remark about me being too much of a loner in front of the other men.

I wanted to be pissed off that, yet again, he was forcing himself into my life, over-complicating our strict work relationship.

But like a fool, I was waiting outside of the house at 3:30 PM on the dot. I waved goodbye to Mike and Chris as Miguel pulled over. His truck was parked on the other side of the road.

"Come on," Miguel chirped from the driver's seat, all smiles.

Suppressing the urge to roll my eyes, I got inside his F-150, having to pull myself up and in with some effort. I was tall, but it was still a huge truck, so it took me a second to get settled.

"Where are we heading?" he asked, even as he started pulling off.

I scrambled to put in the directions before replying, "Norton Automotive. On the other side of town. Where Downton and three other neighborhoods meet, not too far from…"

Trailing off, I stopped myself from saying close to where I lived. He didn't need to know all that.

He nodded, and that was that as the robotic voice guided us along. An awkward pause persisted until we reached a red light a little ways down the road.

"So…," he began, eyes shifting towards me and then back to the road, "what happened to your car?"

Here we go again with twenty questions.

"I got into an accident on the highway. Got it towed, and it's been sitting in the shop this whole week. I figured they'd get to it sooner, but they've been busy and I've been busy with all of this."

I waved towards the window, nudging my head in the direction of Winchelsea House. I did my absolute best to hold back any snark. Despite not getting off to a good start, Miguel was doing *me* a favor. The least I could do was be grateful.

We rode in silence again, exiting the gated community and the posh, rolling country club hills until we hit more typical surroundings. After an equally long, but less awkward pause, Miguel chimed in again to fill the long stretch of silence.

"I see. Well, I'd be happy to give you a ride to and from work until you can get a new ride."

"You don't have to do that," I replied, a little uncomfortable with that arrangement.

It would save me a lot of headache, and money, but that also meant Miguel showing up at my doorstep bright and early for a few weeks, minimum. That was if my car was totaled.

He seemed unfazed, pressing the issue. "But think about

it. We work for the same company. We're both early birds. And I'm happy to do it. Things between us are a little... Um..."

"Tense?" He sucked his teeth in response, and I couldn't help but grin.

He was open, friendly, but didn't seem to like conflict. That or talking about the hard stuff made Miguel as uncomfortable as us spending more time together did for me. Though, the more I stewed on it, maybe *uncomfortable* wasn't the right word.

Vulnerable was more like it. It took a lot for me to expose my issues to someone. It felt like we were moving too fast from strangers to something like—

"... friends."

"What was that?" I asked, catching the tail end of his sentence.

"I said you're right, but I really don't want things between us to be so tense. We don't have to see eye-to-eye on everything, but I hope we can be something close to friends. I mean, we're going to be working together on more projects, hopefully. Why add to the stress?"

He made some very good points. I supposed we would be working together for quite a while. I was hired on as a contractor but would love steady work with Smithson Construction.

This gig was paying very well because of my connection to the client, but it wouldn't last forever, and my cost of living had gone up significantly.

Work out here in California was abundant, especially when you had a good crew of men and a competent project manager. God only knew how much I needed stability as of late.

"You sure it wouldn't bother you to chauffeur me around?"

He lifted a dark eyebrow at me. "I'd like to think of it as

being your guide. There's a lot to do in Gaynor. People to meet. Places to see. And it's better to take it all in when you're not alone."

I shifted in my seat, unsure if he was making a pointed statement. But I knew logically he wasn't. Miguel knew as much about me as I knew about him, which wasn't much past brief formalities. My thumb and pointer finger instinctively reached for my ring finger to twist my band. But it was no longer there. I finally took it off the same time I changed Denise's name in my phone.

Scratching the stubble on my chin, I murmured, "Yeah. Better not to do it alone. If you're offering, I guess there's no point in refusing until I can get back on my feet."

A sense of relief washed over me to relinquish a little bit of control and lean on somebody, anybody for a little while. Even Miguel.

His eyes narrowed in my direction, a curious glint in those moss green depths. But this time he didn't overstep, simply nodding as we eased into a comfortable silence at last.

"Here it is," Miguel said, pulling into Norton Automotive's driveway.

"Thank you," I said, letting *for everything* go unsaid.

He seemed to understand by the way he gave me a quick slap on my shoulder as if to say, "It's okay."

It struck me that we had a full conversation rather than an argument as I slipped out of his truck and walked inside.

Inside were three men, and I approached the one with "Jake" written on his coveralls. The one I'd talked to over the phone.

"Are you Demetrius?" he asked as I walked up to the counter.

"Yes."

His slight frown softened, like he was about to deliver some bad news.

Jake fixed his dark gaze on me and said without ceremony, "I'm sorry to say but your car was totaled in the accident."

"Totaled," I repeated, in a bit of a daze, as if our conversation earlier in the day never happened.

He'd said it was bad, potentially unfixable. But I just ignored that and prayed somehow they'd find a way.

I guess a part of me wanted to believe the answer would be totally different once I came in.

Jake wiped some non-existent dirt from his hands and repeated, "It would cost more than that car is worth to fix it—if making it road-worthy again was even possible. Wish I had better news for you, but your insurance company can help you more than we can at this point."

The rest of what he said was drowned out by a low buzzing in my ears. I moved mechanically across the shop, signing paperwork, and shooting an email to the car rental company about canceling my reservation, before taking a second to sit down in the lounge.

I knew Miguel was waiting, but I needed a moment to collect my thoughts. I scrolled through my phone.

Denise had left a message: "U good?"

A missed call. Then, another text made my phone buzz.

Denise: Car Emoji?

I smiled. She texted worse than our son, never in full sentences. We were young, but she was a technophobe, so preferred to talk on the phone rather than text until recently. It took me two years to convince her to upgrade her five-year-old phone. But then Meechie got her into sending emojis, and now her messages were barely legible hieroglyphics.

Demetrius: I'm good. But the car is totaled.

Denise: Shock Emoji! Need $ for rides?

My mouth twisted upward. I didn't know how long it would take to get my insurance check. But Miguel had offered to be my guide, and I decided then and there I'd take him up on it.

I convinced myself it would save on gas, rideshares, and cabs. Or, the most expensive of all, a long-term rental. A win-win-win-win. And maybe I could start making new friends, building a new life in this town in the process.

Demetrius: I'm good, really. Thank you.

A series of dots started typing. Stopped. And finally started back up again before she sent her last message.

Denise: Blushing Smiley Emoji. Ok.

A part of me felt a little bitter, seeing as that was all she could muster. She was acting a lot more normal than me.

I couldn't lie to myself. I had gotten my hopes up that maybe we could get back together once she came to San Diego. Especially during the first week when we were on the phone constantly, coordinating Meechie's new schedule, the sale of our old house, and everything in between.

Maybe Denise's new job as a real estate agent was taking up so much time she didn't have a lot for me.

Though, I knew that was unfair. She was just acting as I begged her to act once we signed the papers, like everything was normal. And it wasn't like I was unaware of the fact that being together wouldn't mean our romantic feelings would suddenly come bursting back.

So what right did I have to allow that bitterness to turn into anger? I breathed in deep, hearing my tele-therapist in my mind.

A broken car wasn't the end of the world. Nor was a failed marriage. My therapist would warn me I was being obsessive, misdirecting my negative emotions onto others so I didn't have to deal with them head-on.

It was the thing that imploded my otherwise happy marriage with my best friend. Always finding fault in others, and not taking the time to really self-examine. Always too busy providing what I thought was needed, instead of listening to what was really needed instead.

The more I thought about it, I wasn't angry at Denise or this shitty situation. No, I was angry that somehow, someway, all roads lead back to me as the cause of my happy life crumbling away.

When you're a dad, you learn to put your responsibilities first and your feelings last.

As cliché as it sounded, I didn't have the best father figure growing up. He was a hard-ass workaholic, and I inherited the workaholic gene it seemed. But there was one thing my dad constantly drilled into my head, and I truly believed in.

Parents put themselves last. For the kids. For a happy home, and hopefully life.

Work hard.

Keep your head down.

Stay the course.

Do the right thing.

Be better than the best.

Doesn't matter if you're unhappy and unconsciously letting it leak out in every interaction with your wife and kid. Stay together if only for appearances because a two-parent household is best.

Responsibilities first, and feelings last.

So what happens when those emotions well up and threaten to suffocate you? How do you handle your responsibilities when you can barely keep yourself together?

Dad never taught me that part, but life sure as hell was trying to stress test my response by dumping load after load on my shoulders.

I didn't know how to handle the sudden feelings surging inside of me. I was tired of feeling this way. So I did what I always did when I felt overwhelmed. I pushed the rebellious urge down, the feeling of wanting to break down, and tried my best to "fix it."

Which meant carrying my ass back to Miguel's truck, helping Meechie with his homework tonight while he and Denise video chatted, and getting to bed so I could be up bright and early tomorrow. Rinse and repeat.

I walked out of the shop with my shoulders squared and chin raised up. But as I slipped inside Miguel's truck, I sucked in a sharp, shaky breath.

I quickly tried to school my expression, but I knew my vulnerability was leaking out. The urge to whine like a child welled up inside of me. And I hated myself for it.

"Is everything all right?" he asked as I put in the directions home and placed my phone on his phone mount.

"It will be. If you don't mind, could you drive me home?"

I could've punched myself, hearing the sound of my voice wobble. Grown baby. A totaled car wasn't the end of the world, I reminded myself. But even I knew it wasn't the car being totaled that was making me act this way.

"Of course."

Simple. Friendly. Open. And, most importantly, not being nosy. All things I desperately needed at that moment. With a deep sigh, I turned my head towards the window, crossing my arms over my chest as my heart thudded against my ribs.

And I allowed myself to let go, if only a little bit, and see where life took us in this odd attempt at being co-workers and friends.

CHAPTER 6

MIGUEL

I GLANCED AT DEMETRIUS AS WE CROSSED INTO NORTON Heights. For a second there, Demetrius had seemed different, almost… soft, like someone who needed to be protected.

It was a weird juxtaposition of his personality and my instinct. In one way, he was cold and terse, but suddenly I wondered if that personality was used as a wall.

And of course, now I intrinsically wanted to break through it to see what was on the other side.

But he was sitting stoically, looking out the window as though nothing was wrong, as though he hadn't looked completely distraught by his car being totaled, as though that meant his whole life was falling apart.

"Take a look at that," I said. Hoping to pull him out of his thoughts, I pointed out the sky above. "The benefit of an oceanside town is definitely the sky."

"The sky?" Demetrius repeated, amused.

"Oh yeah," I said, watching his gaze fix on the pink and orange clouds. "The sunsets are beautiful from anywhere in the city, but the sunrises are even better."

I felt him watching me and glanced over, catching his gaze for a moment before he looked away.

"When do you find time to watch the sunrise?" he mused after a moment. "Actually, when does *anyone*?"

"Almost every morning," I chuckled. "Before work."

When I looked at him this time, he was gaping, and I couldn't help but laugh.

"You're joking."

I shook my head.

"No, the pier is on my way to work, and I take my breakfast and sit there."

His eyes widened.

"I can't remember ever taking the time to watch the sun set *or* rise. Of course, mornings are pretty busy when you have to get ready for school…"

He drifted off.

Curiously, I glanced at him. He was looking out the window, gaze still fixed on the sky above.

"Did you just recently graduate?"

"Huh?"

I wanted to pry, but my directions app rudely interrupted by saying that we had arrived at our destination.

I pulled up to his address with interest. Norton Heights wasn't as upscale as some of the neighborhoods in Gaynor Beach, but it was still upper middle class. The homes here were nice, clean, and the people were friendly. It was exactly the type of place where you would want to raise a family. Dan had lived around the block and I'd always liked the vibes around here, though I had never seen Demetrius around. Demetrius' place was one of the smaller homes, but it was beautiful, with solid white siding, black trim, and artfully done millwork. Somehow, it suited him, even though he didn't seem like he would be the friendliest of neighbors.

Case in point, he didn't even say goodbye. He wasted no time opening the door and climbing out, almost as though he couldn't wait to get away from me despite the somewhat friendly conversations we'd had.

At the last moment, he paused and bent down to look at me.

"Thanks," he muttered, but then, something else caught my eye. Something that had my jaw dropping. The door behind him opened and a small person popped their head out.

"No way! You have a kid!" I exclaimed.

Why that made my heart soar the way it did was no mystery. I was already achingly lonely with Dan's family now gone.

I didn't want to replace them or anything, but I was still out of the car and marching up the walkway well before Demetrius could even follow what was happening.

"Hey there!"

I couldn't help a huge grin as the startled kid took the hand I offered and shook, looking confused.

"I'm Miguel, your dad's friend from work."

"Oh."

He glanced over at his dad for confirmation.

Demetrius had just reached my side and nodded to his son.

"This is my son Demetrius, Meechie for short."

The similarities were uncanny, right down to that same judgmental eyebrow quirk.

"Meech is better…"

I laughed.

"Man, you two are so alike."

Meech frowned and I bit my lip.

"Sorry, I know, no kid wants to be compared to their parents, right? But don't worry, you're lucky with those genetics."

Demetrius cleared his throat.

"Alright, well, thanks for the ride."

"What happened to the car?" Meech asked.

Demetrius shook his head.

"It can't be fixed."

Meech's frown deepened.

"So, I have to keep walking?"

"For now, yeah. Gaynor Elementary's only around the block."

"Yeah, but I don't know anyone..."

Surprised, I cut in.

"Oh, did you guys just move to Gaynor?"

"Yeah," Meech said, even though I had asked his father. "The middle of nowhere."

My brows shot up.

"What? No! This place is the best! And you came at the best time of year!"

Suddenly I was on a roll, describing all that the town had to offer.

"It's the friendliest place on earth," I said. "There are so many nice small businesses owned by locals, an independent cinema that plays really fun, obscure movies, a drive-in. On the water, there are boat rentals, kayaking, windsurfing, you name it. And we go all out for holidays here. The Fright Night is amazing, and the Autumn Festival is unreal. There's games, bands, you name it. There's even a parade."

Meech actually looked interested and suddenly, I couldn't leave it at that.

"You have to let me take you."

Meech looked up at Demetrius. Despite being in the age group where kids liked to pretend that they were too cool to be interested, there was hope in his eyes and suddenly, it hit me how lonely the two of them must be.

Demetrius sighed and nodded.

"Sure, if you don't mind."

He glanced at me, looking almost nervous, and a warmth settled over me.

"No worries," I insisted. Then, as an afterthought, I added, "You can bring anyone you like, maybe your mother?"

Meech swallowed and shook his head.

"No, she stayed in Bethesda."

I heard the note of bitterness in his voice loud and clear.

"Ah," I said, offering him a sympathetic smile even as a small, selfish tendril of pleasure filled me.

Demetrius wasn't married; he was probably single. They'd just moved here after all and—none of that mattered because we worked together, and he was most likely straight.

I hadn't gotten any interested vibes off of him, at the very least.

Still, I reminded myself, *having another friend would be just as worthwhile.*

"Just us boys then," I said. "We can hit the Autumn Festival."

Demetrius nodded, and Meech seemed to inflate a little, a smile lifting his lips.

"Thanks Miguel," he said.

I reached out and patted his shoulder.

"No, thank you. I can't wait!"

He grinned.

When I looked at Demetrius, he was watching me oddly, but he quickly blinked and smiled.

"See you tomorrow," he said. "Thanks again for the ride."

"Anytime," I said, and then just as I was about to leave, I paused and found myself turning back to him. "You're on my way. I can come to get you in the morning."

He blinked.

"That's not necessary."

I grinned.

"I know it's not necessary."

"Oh."

I raised my brows, still smiling.

"Seven?"

He nodded mutely and I went back to my car, feeling lighter than I had all week.

CHAPTER 7

DEMETRIUS

"Thank you, professor. I promise I won't let you down." I peeked out a hole that would become a window soon enough as a delivery crew placed newly ordered flooring on large tarps outside.

The charred wooden planks, a Japanese method called shou sugi ban, would give Winchelsea House a modern feel using a traditional method, one that had caught on all across California.

"Don't worry," Professor Furukawa's voice chided on the other end of the line, "I trust you, Demetrius. I wouldn't recommend you for a project of this magnitude if I didn't believe in your talent. Just be sure everything is perfect in the basement. When my grandsons are born, I want to turn part of it into a nursery for them."

I nodded at that, watching as Miguel, Mike, and Chris hauled the wood inside, turning away quickly as soon as Miguel and I locked eyes.

Somehow he always seemed to know when I was looking his way. And I found myself sneaking glances more than I would've liked to admit in those days.

We'd been riding in together all week, and as odd as our

arrangement was, it was for the best. Thank God I got gap coverage, despite Denise insisting when I brought it that it was a waste of money.

I was a safe driver, so in her mind, it was a waste of money. And I was, with no accidents on my record since I got my license. Until that mattress went flying through the air, that is.

So I was thankful for Miguel, for being generous with his time while I waited for my insurance to pay me out. Without that pending check, I'd be ass out for months as I scrambled together enough money to get a new car while keeping a roof over our heads.

"Of course, of course," I finally said, coming back to the conversation. "I know that. It's just that I want to deliver the very best. For you, your daughter, and your grandchildren. It means the world that you trust me."

And I really meant it, not just because this project was keeping me afloat post-divorce. No, it was because I respected the professor more than any man I'd known other than my own father.

Hiroshi Furukawa was a world-renowned architect who had somehow ended up teaching at the School of Architecture, Planning & Preservation at the University of Maryland during my sophomore year.

I ditched my would-be career in biomedical engineering after attending one of his lectures and never looked back.

Much to my dad's dismay, though, he still paid my bills through graduate school, which I would be forever thankful for.

The professor made architecture come alive in a way that moved my soul. If I had it my way, I would have probably gone into history and preservation work proper, but there was no way my dad would allow me to pursue a career outside of STEM on his dime, so architectural preservation and restoration became my life.

And now my favorite professor was saving my life once again, soon-to-be-retired in the same town if Smithson Construction stayed on budget and on time.

"You always deliver your best. I've never known you not to," he reassured me in his soft yet stern voice, coughing slightly, sounding out of breath.

I frowned, worried. I had heard bits and pieces of why he was moving out to California, and effectively retiring in his early fifties. Something about a recent sickness and wanting to be closer to his daughter, Sara, was what got back to me.

Hiroshi's wife had passed away years ago, and he had become a shell of himself for a while. I hoped he wasn't terminally ill or something, though I realized that was most definitely not the case. He wouldn't hide something that serious from me.

I hoped, anyway.

But whatever had made him sick was bad enough he decided to pick up and leave the east coast behind too, back to the state where he grew up.

So I truly doubted he had one foot in the grave or something. Besides, he'd have to stay strong for the babies at least. And I could hear it in his voice, that the imminent birth of his twin grandsons, his first grandchildren, was making him happier, too.

Though, like me, he was a workhorse, so he was going to work part-time to keep himself busy. I had no doubt about that. Which was probably why he wasn't concerned about how much we sunk into the house. It was for his daughter's and grandsons' pleasure, more than his.

I wanted to ask the professor exactly what was going on but stopped myself, saying goodbye and hanging up.

I didn't want to pry if he didn't want to tell me. And I'd find out soon enough once he came to town.

"How did it get so late?" Tapping my watch, I plopped down in my chair.

Installing the steps had been trickier than I imagined, and I'd somehow pored over designs all afternoon, even skipping lunch.

I could hear Miguel in my ear saying that I should eat, even imagining his head peeking through my door, thermos in hand, telling me to come to join the guys for a drink later tonight.

They had to be pretty busy, too, for him not to have come in to check on me.

"Hmm… So he decided not to be nosy the same day I needed him to be."

Tapping my pen against the desk, I wondered how the hell I got so entangled in Miguel's life.

Our morning rides had turned into constant invites, especially since he found out I had a kid and was single.

And it wasn't like my insurance check would be in the mail any time soon. That meant anywhere from a few weeks to a whole month before I could even start the process of buying a new car.

There was no way around it.

Which meant we'd be seeing each other practically 24/7.

Though, for some inexplicable reason, that didn't annoy me as much as it should've.

It actually made me think. I didn't know anyone out here, and arranging for a babysitter was proving harder than I had hoped.

If Miguel was willing—and dear Lord did he make it obvious that he was willing—we could do something after work with Meechie. And later, when I could get someone to watch him, go out with Miguel, Mike, and Chris. Just so he would stop inviting me to everything under the sun.

I could even meet another non-work friend there and expand my horizons in the process.

He'd said something about an Autumn Festival. I sucked my teeth, debating if it was really worth it to attend. Meechie would probably love it, the festival would be kid-friendly, and for what it was worth, my son seemed to like Miguel during their first meeting.

He asked about him from time to time, curious. Which was good.

Miguel had a way of forcing himself on you, and it would get Meechie out of his shell. Maybe some kids from school would also be in attendance, which was a win-win-win for me.

But I was already asking a lot of a co-worker, not a true friend. Yet, anyway. Wouldn't I be a jackass to make him ferry us around after hours, on top of morning rides, seeing as Miguel never mentioned bringing his kid along?

If he even had a kid. I figured he had to have one at his age. And the fact that he would want to hang out with a single dad.

"Whatever. Doesn't hurt to ask."

Packing up quickly, I flung my computer bag over my shoulder and wiped off my glasses. They always seemed to be covered in sawdust or other microscopic junk floating in the air.

Once outside, I waved goodbye to the guys, self-conscious at the way they passed glances at me, slapping each other on the shoulder and laughing loudly.

I knew they were most likely talking about hitting up a bar after work, but I had the distinct impression they were talking about me. Or, more likely, us.

I nodded towards Miguel as he pulled up, all smiles, smelling faintly of oak. A rich smell that suited him. I breathed in deep and sighed.

Before I could stop myself, I found myself smiling back.

"So… about the Autumn Festival," I said as I slipped into the passenger seat of his truck, which was becoming a routine.

He perked up instantly. "What about it?"

"Do you mind... um..." I fiddled with a misaligned button on the end of my shirt, rebuttoning it in the process before strapping in. "Would you mind taking my son and me tonight? Would be nice to get out of the house for once. Plus, it's Friday. Maybe you could bring your kid or kids, and they can all play together. Though, I'm not sure if they'd be older than him... Wait...do you even have a child?" I asked absently.

He didn't respond, expression twisted and weary.

Shit!

Maybe I asked something I shouldn't have. I never rambled like that and was usually much more direct. I feared I was picking up Miguel's bad habits.

"I don't have any kids. But I'd love to take you two there."

All I could do was nod, texting Meechie not to walk home from school, before putting the directions to Gaynor Elementary into Google Maps, placing it on the dashboard so Miguel could get there.

I wasn't stepping on that landmine, the reason he didn't have kids. Miguel could simply not want them, or it could be something much worse. So I focused on the long stretch of road between Winchelsea House and my son's school instead.

When we arrived, Meechie was already waiting by the side of the road, wearing yet another oversized hoodie, this one jet black, in this hot-as-Satan's-toenails heat. And then he had the audacity to wear shorts and sandals with socks. I was starting to believe he was immune to the changing weather.

"How was your day?" I asked as he climbed into the backseat. He struggled a bit, the truck being twice the size of my Honda Civic. RIP.

"Okay. I was able to join the soccer team. And art class was fun," he said, his eyes on the back of Miguel's head as he pulled off. "Are we going to that festival?"

I wanted to say stop being rude, but Miguel took it in

stride, grinning as he peeked at him through the back mirror. "Your dad didn't tell you?"

"Well, Mr…" I drifted off as Miguel shot me a strange look, and I realized I didn't know his last name. "*Miguel* is taking us to the Autumn Festival."

"Hmmm…" My son seemed to ponder over his words for a while before shrugging. "Cool."

It was a better response than I expected. I wondered why Miguel knew so much about it. He said he didn't grow up here, and I doubted a single man would willingly go to such a family-friendly, PG-focused event like that willingly.

Which, again, was strange, seeing as he didn't have kids. Maybe he had a sister or brother and took his nieces and nephews every year. I had to believe so, not sure if it was my place to ask.

Recently, I'd been on the receiving end of innocent questions that hit on some deep-seated frustrations. So I figured I'd keep things light and airy, much like Miguel's personality, as we hit the road.

———

ONCE WE ARRIVED, I WAS PRETTY SURPRISED BY WHAT I SAW. I expected a rinky-dink little pumpkin patch with some over-worked food vendors and a hay ride or two. Instead, it was a fun mix between a carnival, a county fair, and a city-sponsored "not-Halloween-in-name" party.

And my son seemed to feel the same. He pulled out his headphones, wide eyes scanning the fairgrounds with excitement.

I smiled, his excitement infectious. When he was younger, little things used to make him happy. But lately, he'd been too cool to hang out with me, let alone at something "for kids."

"What should we do first?" I asked, glancing towards Miguel, who was grinning ear to ear.

"Ring toss?" Miguel offered, so we followed him towards it.

The ring toss was fall themed as well, a nice treat. On the ground were green and brown leaves, with stacks of hay divided in half, coming together in a perfect triangle. Three pumpkins were on the lowest bales of hay, six in total. Four on the next level, two on the next, with one at the tippy-top of the pile.

A vendor came over, dressed as a scarecrow with matching makeup, a Raggedy Ann–themed wig on her head. She handed my son and Miguel three rings, then tried to offer some to me. I went to shake my head no; I would much rather take pictures to save the memory and send to the family group chat. But both Meechie and Miguel insisted, nudging me to join them.

"Okay, fine," I said as I took my stack of green, yellow, and red rings.

"The rules are simple. Get as many rings on the pumpkin stems as you can. The higher you go, the bigger the prize. Who's up first?"

Meechie visibly hesitated, though he looked like he really wanted to try. Before I could respond, Miguel stepped up. Like a pro, he landed his first toss on the highest stem, eliciting some claps and hooting from the other families waiting in line. But then his second toss landed lower, on the first bale of hay. And he missed his last toss.

"Congratulations! Take this ticket to the prize counter for your very own scarecrow pumpkin doll!"

I wasn't sure what kind of abomination a scarecrow pumpkin would look like, but if it was like everything else at the festival, it would be cute rather than creepy.

Miguel took the ticket and slipped it into his back pocket, leaning down to clasp Meechie's shoulders.

"Think you can beat that?"

"Yeah, I can!" he nearly shouted back, determination burning in his gaze.

He was bringing out Meechie's competitive side, which was hilarious to watch. I could tell Miguel had held back, but he wasn't going super easy on him either. The perfect balance.

One of his eyes squinted as he tried to line up his throw. I quickly pulled out my phone. Unfortunately, Meechie missed the first two, but landed the last one on the stack just below the grand prize. We cheered, and I bit my lip to hide my smile. The scarecrow attendant offered Meechie a ticket to redeem for a smaller toy and a bag of candy.

I was up next. I tossed my first two rather quickly, going for low hanging fruit. However, Miguel cleared his throat as I went to toss my last so we could get to see the rest of the sights. I turned to him with a quirked eyebrow. His eyes shot over to Meechie and back. After following his pointed gesture, I could see Meechie's eyes were looking up at me, hopeful I could get the biggest prize for him no doubt.

Sighing, I focused, chewing my tongue a bit, and tossed the ring. It landed perfectly on top of Miguel's ring spinning for a while before settling. More clapping, another grand prize ticket, and a very happy ten-year-old later, I was glad I listened to Miguel.

We weaved our way around the festival until the sun was starting to set, playing games with loads of laughter and more than a little shoving here and there. The amber lighting matched the mood of the festival as we made our way to the end.

"So, what should we do next?" I asked, eyeing a candy apple stand.

I resisted the urge to check my watch, a little worried seeing as it was getting late.

Miguel seemed to track where my gaze landed since he nudged me. "Candy apples? My treat."

Meechie nodded, practically sprinting towards the stand. I

had to snatch him back as Miguel ordered on our behalf. He got two covered in candy—way too damn sweet. But mine was perfect.

He offered me one covered only in caramel sauce as we found a bench to eat on. I took it, savoring the sweetness and the tenderness of the moment too.

Miguel dragged his fingers through his hair, and for once I really saw him. And, as shocking as the thought was, I found him to be rather handsome. Thin crow's feet pinched the corners of his eyes, the only thing really indicating how much of an age gap we had between us.

The sun caught his irises, and they glowed the color of honey with flecks of green. Were his eyes always that color? Hazel, not moss green?

I couldn't remember clearly; I didn't think we'd been so close. Or, more accurately, I didn't think I'd been so relaxed around him. I found myself sneaking glances his way, teeth and tongue sticky with caramel as he and my son chatted away.

Our marriage counselor warned me that kids always bore the brunt of a divorce. It was why Denise and I did everything we could not to split up. Seeing Meechie genuinely happy was all I could ever ask for. And as much as I didn't want to admit it, I had Miguel to thank for that.

CHAPTER 8

MIGUEL

I COULD FEEL THE EVENING COMING TO A CLOSE AND I WASN'T ready.

While we ate candy apples, Meech was going on about his classes, how he had already covered his current science unit at his last school and he was bored out of his mind at school. He had already met a couple of people that he talked to during classes, particularly a kid he was working on a history project with and the girl that sat next to him in English.

I could feel Demetrius' intense focus during the entire conversation, but he wisely stayed out of it.

"It sounds like it's going good," I said gently, aware that Demetrius was listening.

Meech shrugged, biting another chunk out of his apple—caramel dipped in M&M's.

When he swallowed it down, he muttered, "It's okay I guess. I still wish I was at my old school though."

Glancing over the top of his head surreptitiously, I noticed the subdued look in Demetrius' eyes. He was gazing blankly off into the distance, but his brows were lightly drawn together, his lips downturned.

To bide time, I took a bite of my apple. It was caramel too, dipped in marshmallows and chocolate chips.

"You just need a distraction," I said as my gaze landed on the leaf dunk. "Both of you do. Come on!"

I grabbed each of them by the hand, dragging them after me and tossed the last of my apple into a bin we were passing.

The second Meech's gaze landed on the enormous pile of leaves and the seat balanced above it, his eyes lit up.

"Dad first," I said, giving Demetrius a push.

Meech howled with laughter.

"What? I don't think so."

"Dad, I'm going to knock you in!" Meech said, and Demetrius obviously didn't have the heart to turn him down when he looked so happy, because he gave me a half-hearted glare and went to the end of the line. There was only one couple ahead of us. When the girl swung a perfect overhand throw directly at the bullseye mark and her boyfriend toppled dramatically into the leaves, Demetrius visibly stiffened while Meech laughed.

"Oh, I can't wait for this!" he exclaimed.

"Hey, don't have too much fun," Demetrius warned. "I still make your lunches. You hit that bullseye and it's sardines for the week."

Laughing, I reached out, massaging his tense shoulders roughly and then giving him a shove when the girl running the game waved us forward.

"We each want a turn," I said.

"Sure thing. Whoever's first can climb up."

Biting his lip nervously, Demetrius climbed the ladder and perched atop the chair, already clinging to the edges.

"You get two throws," the girl said, offering us each a ball.

It was an easy throw, but I tossed the ball into the air, making a show of measuring the distance.

"Get on with it," Demetrius grumbled.

Oh, how I would love to knock him down, but no, this was Meech's treat. Still, I threw on an evil smile and threw hard.

Demetrius flinched from head to toe and then laughed, whooping loudly when my ball swung just past the target.

"Haha!"

"My turn," Meech said, completely focused.

He took the ball and, with the precision I'd been hoping he had, he swung his arm in an arc, throwing the ball perfectly square in the bullseye.

It hit the metal target with a loud clunk and there seemed to be a moment where Demetrius' eyes widened before the floor and his seat dropped away.

He fell in a floppy mess, getting buried as the trampoline covered in leaves caught him.

Meech cheered far harder than any child should cheer their parent falling and then, for the first time since Demetrius entered my life weeks ago, the man let out a huge guffaw of laughter. The sound was loud, free, and completely contagious, and we were all laughing by the time he straightened, looking a charming mess with his glasses askew and leaves atop his head.

He was still grinning ear to ear when he climbed out of the mess, dusting the leaves off.

"You're next!" he said ominously to his son, pointing a finger to his chest. The effect was ruined by the bright, open smile on his face.

Meech climbed the ladder and sat atop the chair, clearly trying to keep his cool, but I could see how fast his chest was rising and falling.

"Should I?" I asked quietly. "Or you?"

Demetrius' lips pursed.

"Shit," he muttered. "I know he'll have fun, but I just don't have the heart."

"What are you whispering?" Meech asked suspiciously.

I smiled at him.

"Oh, nothing," I said, feigning innocence. "We're just trying to figure out how to catch you off guard."

"You can't—" he started and I threw the ball as fast as I could, catching him mid-sentence.

He squealed as he fell, hitting the leaves with a big bounce and then lying back in them, laughing.

"Oh, I'm so gonna get you," he informed me as he climbed out.

I laughed and climbed up the ladder, taking my seat. It *was* a little unnerving from up here. Even though the distance down wasn't far, not knowing how you would fall or when made the heart race.

I loved things like this though. I loved the exhilaration and anticipation of the unknown, the adrenaline rush. I hoped they hit the target.

Sure enough, they did, choosing to throw their balls at the same time so that they would both "get the pleasure."

It was hilarious and also adorable to watch father and son looking up at me with that same mischievous expression in their eyes.

When the target was hit and the floor fell from under me, I yelped and hit the leaves, laughing as I was bounced. My heart was racing, blood rushing with life, and I didn't know if it was from the game or from everything else.

Being with Demetrius like this, playing with his kid, enjoying the festival. It was different than how it had been with Dan's family. It felt more meaningful somehow, although I couldn't quite place why. It wasn't like they were really mine. Demetrius wasn't my partner, Meech wasn't my kid.

I barely even knew either of them, but somewhere deep inside me, it felt like we all fit. Like a perfect family unit.

I shook the sudden thought out of my head, then physically shook all the leaves free before rejoining them.

"That was so much fun!" Meech said. "When I fell, I thought it was going to be a lot farther."

"I know. You screamed," Demetrius said.

"I did not!"

"Didn't he?" Demetrius asked, quirking a playful brow at me.

"Sorry bud, you totally did."

He groaned loudly, ready to keep arguing but I stopped in my steps.

"Where are you going?" I asked, suddenly realizing that I had been following Demetrius back towards the parking lot.

"Home?" he said. "It's almost eight."

I shook my head at once.

"What? But we didn't get our prizes and we didn't even listen to the band yet!"

"But—"

"Meech is ten. He doesn't need to be in bed by nine, does he?"

"No, I do not," Meech agreed.

"There you go."

I waited, hoping that Demetrius would agree. Finally, he shrugged.

"Sure, let's go watch the band for a bit."

I veered them in the direction of the prize booth. It was no contest which plushie we would pick. Meech and I both immediately zoned in on the happy scarecrow with the pumpkin head and long green hat. It was weird and cute at the same time. We handed in our tickets and Meech took his baggie of Halloween candy happily. I led them towards the music, which echoed through the park to where the bandstand had been erected.

The area was packed, all the seats at the front taken and people spread out on blankets all over the grass.

"We don't have a blanket," Demetrius said regretfully, as though that was the end of it.

I held out my arms, surprised.

"We have grass," I said. "We don't need a blanket."

He blinked, and then his lips quivered slightly.

"Of course," he said, glancing around.

I found a spot for us right in the middle with enough room to spread out and lie back.

Next to me, Meech sat down, watching the performance and totally soaking it in. On his other side, Demetrius carefully lay down, just like I had.

"There's that Gaynor Beach sky you keep talking about," he said, resting his head on his arms.

I grinned and looked up at it.

The sun was long gone, but the soft indigo and lavender clouds as it darkened were still striking.

"Beautiful, isn't it?"

"Yeah," Demetrius whispered, and something about his voice drew my gaze.

He wasn't looking at the sky. He was looking at me.

"Why are you so good with kids?"

The sudden question immediately brought a smile to my face.

"I love kids," I said. "Always have, but Dan—the PM you replaced. I got really close to him and his family. He has two kids and another on the way, but Perry is Meech's age; Lexi is six. They're both the best."

"Where did they go?" Demetrius asked.

"Back to San Jose to be with Lea's family."

"Hm. Sounds like you miss them already."

"I'm realizing that more and more," I sighed. "I played it off like it was nothing when they were leaving. It's been so long since I had a family. I didn't realize how attached I got to theirs…"

I drifted off, realizing how much I was spilling, and glanced at Demetrius self-consciously.

His expression was soft and warm, full of compassion.

My heart leaped as our eyes met and then, just as quickly, the moment passed. He blinked and looked back up at the sky, watching it silently while the band continued to play artistic covers of songs we all knew.

Eventually, after about the fourth or fifth song ended, he sat up, stretching and I knew I had milked this day long enough.

"Time to go, kid," Demetrius said, patting his son's shoulder.

Meech didn't put up a fight. He seemed tired and suddenly; I felt guilty for pushing them to stay out.

We walked back to the car in companionable silence. The drive was quiet too, but whenever I caught either of their eyes, they both smiled at me.

By the time we pulled up next to their new house, Meech was half asleep in the back. Demetrius reached into the back and woke him with a hand on the leg.

"We're home."

Meech blinked and stretched, yawning.

"Did you have fun?" I asked.

He nodded and smiled at me in the mirror.

"Yeah. Thanks, Miguel."

"No worries," I said.

He climbed out of the car but paused by the window.

"You're still going to take us to the Halloween thing too, right?"

"Fright Night?" I asked, smiling. "Of course."

I waved and wished him goodnight as he climbed the steps to the front door.

Next to me, Demetrius opened the door but remained planted in his seat. He watched Meech until the front door opened and he went inside, then turned and looked at me.

"Thank you," he said. "For everything."

It was too dark to see his face properly, but his voice...

Suddenly, it was all I could do to not lean across our seats and kiss him. Maybe he wanted me to.

I moved, shifted just a little, and suddenly his seatbelt clicked out and he climbed out of the car, not even noticing my attempted advance.

"See you on Monday," he said and, with that, went after his son.

I sat there, mentally kicking myself.

Demetrius was straight, I reminded myself.

Even if he wasn't, getting with him... that wasn't why I was doing this. But there was something about him that drew me in. Something about Meech, too, made me want to spoil him. I loved kids after all, and I had none of my own. I had never settled down the way that Demetrius had at such a young age. I'd never thought that was what I was missing. A settled, family life.

Yet Demetrius exuded that calm, reliable, steady energy, and I was drawn to it.

Sighing, I started the truck back up and pulled out of the driveway.

After a day full of fun and warmth, I wasn't eager to get to my empty home.

CHAPTER 9

DEMETRIUS

"JOIN A DATING APP?"

I frowned down at my phone, reading a message out loud, as I prepared our lunches. One for Meechie and me, and an extra one for Miguel. The bungalow we'd moved into had a much smaller kitchen than my old home, so I felt like a giant moving around in a plastic dream house.

I added an extra fruit cup to his bag and another slice of meat to Meechie's sandwich since he had soccer practice in the evening. Mondays were always jam-packed, and today was no exception.

My eyes flicked down to my phone on the counter. I didn't know why the simple suggestion was making me so nervous.

"Aye!" I shouted at my son who seemed determined to run out the door faster than the speed of light. "Don't forget your lunch. Or your cleats."

"Already got them. Thank you!" he said, running up to snatch his lunch bag before finally zooming out of the door.

Taking a deep breath, I started texting Miguel not to worry about lunch for work, ignoring the notification until it disappeared. Since Miguel kept refusing gas money for hauling me and Meechie around, and had also treated us to the candy

59

apples, I figured I had to do something to thank him. Making lunch wouldn't pay him back, but it showed I wasn't completely unaware of how much of his time we were taking up.

Right before I could hit send, another notification popped up.

Alonso: I promise. You're too young to stay single for long. Get back out there.

Biting my lower lip, I glanced at the picture of my old roommate from college. Alonso López was a star pitcher on the baseball team, and I was on it because my parents believed in me being an "all-rounder," which meant being involved with sports as well as being a star student since I could remember.

I wasn't very good at any sport, despite being over six foot, and was benched for the majority of my college career. I did like working out though, and being able to skip class because I had to attend games, which made my college sports days a fond memory. Plus, I had always loved seeing Alonso play. He had a passion for it, before he mysteriously dropped out and was never heard from again.

He scraped his social media. Changed his phone number. Everything was gone in an instant. He went ghost. But then, out of the blue, he popped back up in my feed a few months ago, around the time of my divorce.

We reconnected, and I was stunned to find out he had a five-year-old daughter and a boyfriend, of all things. I'd always assumed he was straight from the amount of socks on doorknobs I encountered my freshman year, and women coming in and out of our dorm room.

Not that it mattered to me who he dated. You learn something new about people every day. But when Alonso proceeded to invite me to a group for single fathers once everything went down with me and my ex, I was confused seeing as he had a partner. But I never pried much deeper.

I finally sent my message to Miguel and slipped my phone into my back pocket as I waited for him to arrive.

Something about the festival and returning to an empty bed had stirred up something inside of me. I missed having someone to talk to, to share my life with. I loved my son, but being a parent and a good worker couldn't be everything. Maybe it was because I got married so young, but I got used to being with someone in a house full of life. I wanted that back, badly.

But I really didn't think joining the hookup scene would solve that. Sure, people found love on dating apps all the time, but I sure as hell hadn't. Being a twenty-eight-year-old single father didn't help my chances either.

Besides, I'd done all the post-divorce rebounding I needed for a lifetime. Sex with no strings attached *seemed* amazing after being committed to one person for over a decade. But I couldn't bring myself to go all the way with the women I tried to date after Denise and I broke up.

As corny as it sounded, the emotional connection just wasn't there. And as things disintegrated last year, I made the shocking discovery that it was hard to get my dick up without it, that deeper emotional bond.

Maybe I was self-conscious. Maybe the stress of splitting up caused me to have erectile dysfunction. Who knew! I'd only been with Denise since we were teens. It just felt right with her and wrong with everyone else.

Maybe it was because deep down I wanted more than a good night. A quick, hard fuck every now and then just wouldn't satisfy this deep-seated need. But I didn't know where to start.

Drumming my fingers against the kitchen counter, I thought about asking the guys out for a drink. I didn't have all night; I needed to pick up my son around six or seven, depending on how hard the coach worked them. But I figured if I could become friends with Miguel, it wouldn't be that hard with Mike and Chris.

It was a far cry from joining a dating app or getting a girl-friend, but the more friends I had, the easier this new phase of my life would become. People to hang out with equaled an expanded social circle. And meeting someone I could really connect with and trust with my heart should follow.

A horn honked outside, interrupting my train of thought.

"Oh shit!"

Miguel never honked the horn, which meant I'd been lost in my thoughts. I scooped up our lunches and dashed out, waving with my free hand as I slipped inside of his truck.

"Here," I said, dumping his lunch in his lap.

He gave me a strange look before chuckling. "Thanks. But you didn't have to."

"I wanted to." And that was that.

We drove in companionable silence afterward, the awkwardness long gone. And it felt good as hell to have someone to call a friend on this side of the country for once. And I really did consider Miguel to be a friend, someone to lean on.

Once we arrived at work, I went over the day's plans with the guys and we got to it. We had to finish the walk-out base-ment tonight, by next week at the very latest, to stay ahead of schedule. But as the day dragged on, I found my eyes lingering on Miguel as he moved through the site.

He seemed to notice it too, every once in a while smiling at me. I turned my attention back to Chris, or Mike, or the drying paint on the wall as quickly as I could every time he caught me.

Was I sneaking glances? Was that normal? I mulled over the thought for a moment and discarded it just as fast. I was probably just more aware of Miguel because our relationship had changed so drastically. We were friendly now, so now I noticed him more rather than tried to avoid him the best I could.

But as I ascended the steps to my office, I couldn't stop thinking that I was looking for him more than a supervisor should be seeking out a foreman, especially when I didn't really have anything to say.

I sat at my desk, shoulders tensing as a knock hit the door. I was expecting us to have lunch together, so why was my stomach in knots?

"Hey, come in." I tried to sound neutral.

He pulled up a chair in front of my desk and sat down.

"Thanks for lunch."

"You're welcome." I shifted in my seat, nibbling at my own sandwich and sipping at my water.

"Tuna?" he asked.

"You don't like it?" I said as I took another bite, avoiding eye contact.

"No, it's good," he assured me, as a peculiar twinkle lit up his eyes, counting on his fingers. "Autumn Festival, done. Fright Night next. I've been doing a fantastic job as your guide to Gaynor Beach, haven't I?"

That self-assured cheekiness of his would've had me rolling my eyes less than a week ago. But I couldn't stop myself from smirking.

"Good enough, I guess."

"Well, as thanks for the lunch, how about we go to the pier?"

"The pier?" I leaned back in my chair as he leaned forward.

"Yup. Gaynor Beach pier, smack dab in the middle of downtown. You can actually see Willis Cove and the Marina Park with all these rich folks' yachts docked on a clear day when you look left. And on the right is Willis Point and the lighthouse. It has a ghost story attached to it, maybe even a tour if I remember, but I think you and Meech will love Fright

Night more. You still haven't seen the sunset or the sunrise have you? It's gorgeous. After work, of course."

The tip of my tongue poked from my mouth as I thought about it, as Miguel had a habit of dumping way too much information in one sentence.

It would be nice to go somewhere quiet and remote to unwind for a bit, rather than get stuck in a bar for an hour or two, I supposed. And I could always ask to hang out with everyone else later.

Miguel looked at me with anticipation, and finally I relented.

"Sure. But we have to pick up Meechie by six."

I could see him suppressing the urge to roll his eyes. "Don't worry. We won't stay out *that* late. Just enough to loosen you up a bit and get your mind off this house."

———

WE ARRIVED AT THE PIER ABOUT TWENTY MINUTES AFTER WORK, as traffic was starting to pick up. But once we arrived, I knew instantly it was worth it. Miguel didn't lie for one second when he said the sunset would be gorgeous.

The sky was vibrant, a beautiful rainbow of color stretching out into the far horizon. The cloudless skyline allowed me to see the tip of the cove and the top of the light-house, too, just like he promised.

I took a deep breath as we walked to the edge of the pier. We were alone, which I found rather odd, but I didn't dwell on it. It felt so peaceful, and I wondered how much better witnessing a sunrise would be out here.

"What do you think?" he asked, the wind tossing his hair as he came up beside me after parking.

Miguel lifted his face to the setting sun, the golden rays soaking his tan skin. Once again, I found myself staring at

Miguel versus what was right in front of me. I quickly averted my gaze as he looked my way, clearing my throat.

"Just like you promised. Better, even. I should bring Meech out here some time."

"*We* should," he said with a wink.

I nodded mutely. It was going to be a whole lot of *we* doing just about everything while I waited for my check to arrive in the mail. But as the days passed, I found myself less and less worried about when it came. And more and more curious about getting to know my new friend.

We took a seat on an empty bench and just soaked in the sights. The beach wasn't too far away, and I could already imagine how nice it would be to come down here during summer.

I was still warm enough to swim, which was surprising this late into the year. Though, I reminded myself a beach town on the West Coast would have different weather than I was used to.

The only downside to the beautiful views was the briny air. It lashed at my skin, and I really wished I had some lotion on hand because I knew I was getting ashier by the minute. But I let go of that worry and just tried to *be*.

Be in the moment.

Be present with my joy.

Be with him, and enjoy it.

The last *be* had my face twisting up before I could stop myself. It wasn't wrong to enjoy the company of a friend, so I didn't know why it made me feel... odd to admit it.

Yet, still, it did.

I twisted my empty ring finger, which was becoming a nervous habit.

"It's probably not my place..." Miguel trailed off, hazel eyes drifting down to my hand. "But—"

"I'm divorced." I cut him off, knowing what he was going to ask. It was going to come up eventually.

"Oh." Something in the mood shifted, or maybe we did, coming closer than we were before. "How long were you two together?"

"Years, though it feels like it went by too quickly. And then it all came crashing down about a year ago. We made it official three months ago. And now I'm here."

In that moment, I was happy I had practiced giving this speech. The rehearsed nature of it all made me feel less crappy saying it out loud.

"Years?" Miguel sounded incredulous, which was strange to me.

What did he expect me to say when I had a ten-year-old son at home?

"Since before my son was born so... Huh. Yeah, we would've celebrated ten years this year. We started dating, what, sophomore year of high school? So about twelve years altogether."

For once, Miguel was visibly shocked. I guess he'd assumed I had some oops baby as a teenager and me and his mom split shortly thereafter.

He blinked rapidly, before whispering, "Oh, I see. That's a long time. A long, *long* time. What were you, like sixteen?"

I shrugged. "Yeah. But it was good, for the most part. I don't regret having my son young or getting married young. It made life more... colorful."

I nodded to the sky with a smile, but Miguel still seemed deep in thought, processing how long Denise and I had been together. The way he reacted made me realize how long it actually sounded, seeing as I wasn't that old. Not even thirty.

"Sixteen... Woah. At sixteen... that was when my dad died and I had my first taste of freedom. Sounds terrible, I know, but looking back, I barely knew him. He was obsessed with work and wasn't around much. Then he got sick and I spent two years caring for him. He resented being mostly bedridden and I was the only one he had to take it out on."

"Wow," I breathed, surprised to hear Miguel sharing like this. "It sounds like you had a lot of responsibility early on."

"Not like you," he argued. "Like I said, I felt free at sixteen, like I wouldn't let anything hold me back in life again. When I was your age now, what, twenty-eight? Man, I was backpacking across Asia then. Getting wasted. Having fun. Meanwhile, you've spent all these years taking care of Meech, having a marriage... Can't imagine going to college on top of it all."

I nodded, happy to hear Miguel opening up just like me. I wasn't sure what I expected his life to be like before I met him, but I certainly didn't expect that. Not irresponsible, just so... free. Maybe even a little lonely from my perspective anyway.

"That sounds... wild! Fun. Free. Settling down isn't for everyone. I get it. And trust and believe, it's not like we did it alone. Her parents stopped short of disowning her when they found out we were pregnant. But you wouldn't believe this if you knew him, but my father didn't seem too distraught. He's a hard-ass, I half-expected him to crook."

My eyes drooped, reminiscing, "He just drilled it into my head that I needed to make things right, and man up. Basically get married right away. And I was going to finish school, no matter what. If anything, he took it better than my mama did. Now my mama guilt trips me every other day for moving her grandson so far away. Anyway, they helped us. Ain't no way we could've done it alone. It takes a village, especially when you start a family young."

"So," I said as I turned to him, flinching as his face was closer than I thought. "D-Don't feel bad about not wanting to settle down."

He looked at me for a long time before whispering, "Yeah. But people change. Wouldn't be bad settling down now."

I nodded slowly, and I swore we got closer again, so close Miguel's knee was knocking against mine.

"...Yeah. I wouldn't mind trying again soon. As crazy as that sounds. I thought we could work things out, kind of kept me from looking elsewhere for a while."

His expression turned a little sour, leaning forward, elbows on his knees. "Do you think you can still work things out with your ex?"

I chuckled, and again the hint of bitterness in my voice caught me off guard. Did I still think so? No, no, it was over, and I knew it deep down.

Even the phantom weight of my wedding band had disappeared a long time ago. I reached for it out of habit more than regret or longing. A habit that wouldn't die.

Silently, I pulled out my phone. Miguel felt safe. And he didn't seem to judge. I scrolled down until I reached a picture on my feed. There was nothing overtly obvious from it. Just two co-workers in a real estate office with big smiles, not even standing too close together at that. But to me, all that needed to be said was said when I looked down at her hand.

Empty, like mine.

"Is this your... *ex*-wife?" He seemed to place emphasis on *ex*.

It stung a bit, but sometimes the truth hurt.

"Yup. No ring. And I think a new man. Though she won't tell me until they're probably about to walk down the aisle. We're kind of the same in that way. We want things to be serious before they're known by anybody else. If that makes sense?"

"...Yeah, I get it. Sorry you found out from a picture?"

His voice lifted in question, and I couldn't help but laugh. To normal people, it didn't look like anything. But seeing as Denise was pregnant by the time my folks found out about us, I knew without having to ask who this new man was if she was willing to post a picture with him online.

"It's alright. Honestly, I don't have a right to get angry. It's not like things ended horribly between us. The opposite, really. We just grew up and drifted apart romantically. Everything was work, work, work for me. And she wanted to do more than just raise our son. Go back to school and all."

I gritted my teeth, hoping I wasn't turning this beautiful evening into a therapy session. "You know, a part of me almost wishes it had ended badly. Not because I'm stupid enough to think that would be better. But because it would give me an excuse for still hoping."

"Hoping for what?" There it was again, that strange strain in his voice, like Miguel was suppressing some unspoken emotion.

Maybe what I was saying was hitting a personal note. He had to be in his late thirties or early forties. Though I'd never asked outright. Maybe he'd been divorced too and talking about all this was too much?

"Hoping we can magically fix things and be a happy family again. But I'm over it now. We'll co-parent, and do our thing going forward. Baby steps. I haven't dated in twelve years. I gotta give myself some grace getting back out there. Sorry if I'm being depressing. This beautiful view in front of us and I'm hung up on the past."

"It's not like it's been years since you two split. I understand."

"Have you been divorced before?" I asked.

"No, but I've had my heart broken. So I understand."

The drop in his tone and shoulders clued me in that whoever broke Miguel's heart meant a lot to him. And he was being a little too understanding. I figured I should open the floor for him to vent if that was what Miguel needed to do too.

"Was she your fiancée?" I blurted out without thinking.

He shifted uncomfortably. I had pried too much.

But before I could say I was sorry, he spoke in a whispered voice: "No she wasn't, and I broke things off. But then he really broke my heart, and ever since then I've just done my own thing."

My mouth formed a perfect O, not sure why it shocked me so much that he was…

Gay?

Bi?

He definitely said *he* meant a lot to me, but *she* before that. I clasped my fingers together. Tried not to read too much into it.

Whatever his sexuality might have been, Miguel got me. And that was all that really mattered in the end.

No need to overthink past that.

"I see. Well. There's no point hanging on to the past. We move forward. Which reminds me… You're a good listener. A good friend. I'm sorry we didn't get off to a good start."

"Thank you? And it's okay." Miguel's voice lifted in question again, looking up at me, his moody hazel eyes reflecting mine.

I gulped, in a hurry to change the course and tone of our conversation.

"Sooo… you wouldn't mind trying to hook me up, would you? At some point down the line."

"Come again?" He seemed startled by the question, as uneasiness settled in his shifting gaze.

"Remember? You said you'd be my guide. There's a lot to do in Gaynor. Things to do and see. I'm asking you how a single father in his late twenties meets someone around here? Preferably not at a school-sponsored function. Most of those women have husbands and boyfriends, you know?"

I tried to keep the mood light and airy and figured he'd do the same. Things were getting a little too emotional, pensive, and we came to the pier to loosen up, not get bogged down in bad emotions.

We could hit up some bars. Miguel was single, and I assumed Mike and Chris were too. I hadn't dated in over ten years, and I had stayed faithful. Marrying your high school crush made you ill-equipped to tackle a dating scene that had gone virtual, especially when you had a kid.

But instead of offering up a nightclub, a place to pick up women—he had dated a woman at some point—or preferably someone he knew, Miguel leaned in closer. Too close, actually, so close I could feel his breath ghost against my skin.

"I'm sure it won't be hard to find someone without my help," he said.

"But I'm not really looking for friends with benefits. I'm looking for... something real. I don't know, I feel like it's easier to open your heart to someone you can trust. And I'm too new around here to know who I can trust."

I knew I sounded old fashioned, but it was the truth. Maybe I was just built different, better suited for marriage. But I liked to know someone was home waiting for me, to deal with life with, and live a life that didn't revolve around parenting, work, and school.

Miguel stayed quiet for a long time, pensive, but no longer sullen. Then he looked at me in a way that made my stomach twist into knots again, his gaze too hot, too piercing, and yet I couldn't turn away.

And he was *way* too close.

"There's nothing wrong with having a little fun once in a while. It's just as real, I can promise you that."

Did I imagine it, or did his hand slide across the wood of the bench closer to mine?

"You never know when it can become something more."

"We should get going," I spat out, the tension too much for me to handle.

There shouldn't have been any tension at all. We were just two guys hanging out on a dock. Nothing more, nothing less.

And, yet...

Miguel's eyes flicked down to my watch. "I guess so."

I stood up before I could stop myself, lingering by the

bench as he looked up at me. But this time his gaze was easy, open, *friendly*. Just as it had always been, since we got to know each other. And now that I didn't see him as a nuisance, it felt reassuring for Miguel to look at me that way.

"You should come to hang out with us. I... I mean, Mike, Chris, *and* I are dying to get to know you. Worry about dating some other time. For now, just enjoy a little freedom, hm?"

I nodded, not really sure how to respond. Miguel was a social butterfly while the other two men were gruffer, got shit done, and kicked back after work.

I'd never built up a strong tolerance, or taste, for alcohol. Even back when I did party, which was every blue moon in between work, home life, and school. And the last thing I needed to do was some embarrassing shit like get wasted and cry over my broken marriage and ex.

"Sure. Let's find a time that works, and I'll make sure someone can watch my son."

And with that, I turned stiffly towards the car, feeling his eyes on my back like fire licking at my spine.

I didn't remember getting home. I just found myself desperately looking at the changing scenery, overly aware of Miguel, and how close we felt in such a huge truck. I got out as soon as we got to my house, but stopped short of going inside without so much as a goodbye.

"See you tomorrow," I murmured.

"Don't you need me to pick up Meech?" he asked.

"He can walk," I said, eyes flicking to him and then to his mirror.

"...Alright. But we're still good for Fright Night tomorrow, right?"

"Of course. You, me, and, ah, Meechie. See you."

I tried to sound casual. I hoped I sounded like it wasn't a big deal, because it wasn't.

...*Right?*

As I shut the door, racing inside my house, I couldn't help

reliving that moment on the bench that shouldn't have felt like that.

My jumbled thoughts.

How close he was.

The way the setting sun caught in his eyes.

Strange emotions started welling up inside, too quickly for me to squash.

I didn't dare put a voice to it, but one thing kept swirling around in my mind that entire night—how acutely I wanted him to lean in just a little closer on that bench, and how much I wanted to feel that heated gaze on me again.

CHAPTER 10
MIGUEL

"What is that?" Demetrius demanded the second his front door opened.

"My costume," I said, confused. "Where's yours?"

Before Demetrius could explain away his usual long-sleeved shirt and jeans, Meech stepped out, also in a boring outfit. Jeans and a graphic hoodie. I nearly died.

"What? No! You're the kid! You have to be in a costume too or I look ridiculous."

Meech started laughing.

"You're a police officer?" he asked. "Do you have a gun?"

"No, but I have this very painful plastic baton to whack you with if you act out of line."

"Oh God," Demetrius muttered, looking up. ""Please don't keep up some sort of cop routine all night. I beg of you."

I grinned and waited until he reached the front door of my truck before stopping him.

"Excuse me sir," I said loudly. "It's into the back with you."

I made a very exaggerated effort at pushing him into the

backseat for Meech's entertainment until I got a very, *very* unimpressed look from my prisoner and released him.

"On second thought, you can be my partner."

I winked and opened the front door for him.

Shaking his head, he climbed in.

"Here."

As soon as I was in the driver's seat, I pulled the hat off my head and placed it perfectly atop Demetrius'.

"Do you want the cuffs too?"

His lips parted, no doubt to tell me to shut up and drive when Meech chimed in.

"I'll take them!"

I laughed, unhooked the plastic contraption from my belt, and handed it over along with one of the keys.

"I'll keep the second key in case you lose that one," I said. "With our luck, you'll end up handcuffed to the Ferris wheel or something."

In the backseat, Meech was grinning an evil grin at his new toy.

Preteen boys were truly evil. Adorable, but evil.

I couldn't wait to see his reaction to the haunted houses. Actors in various costumes walked the park, terrorizing visitors. The haunted houses had different levels though. My favorite one was the blackout house. It was pitch black with noise effects. You had to feel around to find exits, but there were actors hiding in the dark to scare you too.

"I don't like this," Demetrius said, watching me. "You look too happy."

Laughter burst from my lips.

"Excuse me?"

"You're up to something."

"No, I'm not," I said innocently.

He raised a brow at me, and I caved.

"Fine! I can't wait to see how scared you get!"

"My dad doesn't get scared," Meech piped up from the back.

"That's only because he has never been to the Gaynor Beach Fright Night."

They both started to argue, but I held firm.

"You're going to scream," I promised. "At least once."

Demetrius gave me an incredulous half smile, and then his eyes narrowed in challenge.

"We'll see," he said. Then, with a mischievous smile I didn't even know he was capable of, he added, "You'll scream."

"Me?!" I laughed. "No way. I love Halloween. None of this stuff scares me."

"We'll see," he repeated ominously.

I wanted to keep the banter going, but we were pulling into the lot and the endless loop of parking-spot searching began.

Eventually, we had to leave and park on a side street nearby before walking back. Not the end of the world, but there was a massive line to enter the park by the time we got there, and then, the moment we were through the doors, Meech waved at some kids excitedly.

They waved him over at once, and me and Demetrius waited while they talked.

The sounds, the atmosphere of autumn and Halloween, were thick in the air. The smell of funnel cake and popcorn, the sounds of spooky music, and people screaming on the rides.

I was eager to show them around but had an idea what was going to happen the second Meech turned back to us with eager eyes.

"Can I go around with them?" he asked. "They're my friends from school."

Demetrius bit his full lower lip, gaze shooting unexpectedly to me for support.

I nodded and he looked at the kids. There were four of them and a parent as well, who waved and smiled, and Demetrius turned to his son, clearly pretending that he wasn't freaking out over sending him around the park alone with people he didn't know. He approached the mother, chatting to her for a minute, and I couldn't help remembering what he'd said at the pier about wanting to date like-minded women. Considering that *this* woman was probably married, I really shouldn't have been feeling strangely threatened. After all, how much more clear could Demetrius have made it? I wasn't what he wanted. And yet, it still *felt* like sometimes he was looking at me like I was what he wanted.

"Do you have your phone?" Demetrius asked Meech, who nodded, bouncing with excitement.

"Call me in an hour, okay? If you don't, I'm sending a search party out."

Meech nodded, already bounding away with his friends.

"Okay, Dad! Bye!"

Demetrius watched him go, looking stunned.

"He couldn't get away fast enough," he sighed miserably.

"It's a good thing," I reminded him, drawing his gaze. "He's making friends. Friends are what make you feel like you belong..."

I drifted off at the look Demetrius was giving me, suddenly seeing the parallels of what I had said. I *had* kind of forced this friendship to form. But that wasn't a bad thing, was it?

"You're so nice," he suddenly said.

I blinked.

"You are. You're nice. Kind. A good person..."

A flutter of warmth spread through me, my cheeks heating.

I didn't know what to say or how to respond to that. I wanted to argue though. I wanted to tell him that I'd only gone out of my way to befriend him because it would make work more enjoyable, but that didn't explain the rides, the shared meals, the trips to the festivals with his son on the weekends.

I liked being around him though, so even that felt a little bit selfish.

Shrugging, I knocked his shoulder.

"Don't get too emotional now just because your son is moving off on his own. There's still a few more years before college."

He rolled his eyes and bumped me in return.

"So, what now?" he asked.

"Now…," I said, a slow smile forming on my lips, "I scare you."

"You're on."

His confidence turned out to be well deserved. Demetrius was like a rock. When one of the girls dressed like a zombie ghost from a horror film who had scared Dan's wife Lea nearly to tears last year walked right up to his face and stared into his eyes, he hadn't even blinked.

The first haunted house was standard, more for kids, with fake-looking displays of body parts and triggers that made things light up or move slightly.

"Okay," I admitted, "that one was weak, but we haven't gone on the wheelbarrow ride yet. Just wait."

"Is that the scariest one?" he asked.

"Well, no. That would be the blackout house—"

"I knew it! You think you'll get me that easily? Let's skip ahead," he challenged.

"You think you can handle it?" I goaded.

"Oh, I can handle it," he said, coming right up into my face, a little too close, the cop hat still perched atop his head brushing my hair.

"Alright," I conceded, my heart suddenly racing.

Grinning, he turned, looking for the signs for the next haunted house.

The blackout house was held in a big tent, erected next to the festival games. While we stood in line, Demetrius started to point out all the kids playing games nearby, asking me where I thought Meech was.

Somehow, I was able to answer all his questions even while I was aware of the way I felt drawn to stand closer to him, to smell his cologne, maybe even close enough to brush the fabric of his shirt.

Something was happening.

I couldn't be entirely sure, but it was hard to completely disregard the increased frequency of lingering looks from those intense, dark eyes. Or the way he turned to me more now, always brushing me when he didn't need to. Touching my arm, nudging me.

My head was screaming at me that Demetrius was straight. All this time I had been sure, but now, one step too close, and I was doubting everything I had been sure of when it came to the other man.

He was so young to have a kid Meech's age. He'd been with Meech's mom since they were teenagers. Who knew themselves fully as a teenager? I sure as hell hadn't. Maybe now that he was single for the first time in over ten years, he was seeing things a little differently.

Maybe I was making him see things differently.

"What are you thinking about?" Demetrius suddenly asked, pulling me from my thoughts.

I swallowed, realizing that I had gone silent for too long. That a frown was plastered across my face.

Shaking myself, I took a moment to think of what to say.

"Just wondering how best to scare you in there."

A grin lifted his lips and the way he smiled at me, so playful and open, made butterflies erupt inside me. What I wouldn't give to kiss that smile.

"You're going to be the one screaming," he said. "Remember?"

It was official; he was far more adorable than he had any right to be. Who knew that buried just beneath that cold wall was such a cute personality?

Finally, it was our turn to enter.

The kid taking the tickets gave us the usual run-through.

"Don't intentionally touch any of the actors. If you're too scared just say so, and someone nearby will escort you out. Enjoy the fright of a lifetime."

Grinning ear to ear, I let Demetrius lead the way.

He entered through the front curtain. The thick plastic of the door blocked out most of the noise and light immediately, but it was when we went through the second that we were properly sealed in darkness and silence.

There was something about the nothingness that sent a thrill of fear through me, despite doing this one every year. The unknown was a terrifying thing.

Next to me, Demetrius didn't move.

"What now?" he asked.

I could hear the tension in his voice and reached out, finding his arm which was taught with discomfort.

"We find our way out," I said, amused.

He shifted away from me, his arms lifting, clearly trying to feel where he was going.

I joined, finding the wall and walking along it, careful to take my time in case I touched something unexpected.

A shuddery gasp to my left had me spinning.

"What is it?" I asked, reaching towards Demetrius.

"Uh. I don't know. Feels like hair."

His back hit my chest, and I held him steady. I could feel his heart racing against my chest.

"It's probably a mop or something," I said, an unexpected surge of pity filling me. "Come on."

I took his hand, pulling him carefully forward.

Suddenly, a low sound reached my ears. A deep, quiet growling from the direction we were heading.

"What is that?" Demetrius asked in a squeak.

"Uh… a dog?" I suggested.

"More like a wolf," he muttered. "Where is it coming from?"

"This way."

Clutching my hand like a lifeline, Demetrius let me lead him towards the creature—which realistically was probably nothing more than a sound recording, but it still was eerie as hell.

I tried to bypass the thing but, suddenly, hit a dead end.

"Shit," I muttered.

"What? What? What?" Demetrius asked anxiously.

"Dead end," I said. "Try to feel for the way out."

"Oh. *Fuck*. Okay."

I appreciated that he wasn't faking keeping his cool this time, but the edge in his voice was freaking *me* out now. We were right by the growling, and suddenly the pitch rose in warning and there was a sudden commotion. Something moved and then something furry barreled into us and we *both* screamed, falling back.

I recovered quickly, but Demetrius was done, still clutching my hand in his as he ran.

Where he was going, I sure as hell didn't know and I doubted he did either. We hit a wall and then suddenly were through a passageway. We tripped a switch that suddenly flashed light at a ghoulish figure in the corner, which turned and grinned at us, heading to the doorway to block us just as we were plunged into darkness again. I knew she was an actress in makeup but the sight of her sent a chill down my spine.

"Oh, fuck no!" Demetrius shouted, rushing forward, taking me with him as the ghoul's fingers scraped against our clothes.

"Ugh!"

I stumbled away from her, and my hand yanked accidentally free.

"Miguel!" Demetrius' anxious voice instantly rang in the air, followed by a shout, and then, he was crashing into me, full-bodied, smacking me flush against the wall and clutching my cop uniform like his life depended on it.

"Someone's in here!" he shouted. "Someone grabbed me!"

"It's okay!"

I grabbed his shoulders, trying to steady him, even though my heart was pounding with fear too. Then, suddenly— because I was stupid and human and he was pressed against me and it seemed like the right thing to do—I kissed him.

His entire body went even more rigid.

For a split second, I stood there, our lips pressed together, wondering how the hell that had even happened, and then, just as shockingly, a noise left him, like relief, and he was kissing me back.

His hands didn't stop clutching my shirt but he tilted his head, deepening the kiss, lips parting like he was hungry for more, and I obliged. I kissed him hard and hungry, just like he wanted, pressing my tongue between his soft lips, tasting him until someone cleared their throat awkwardly next to us.

Demetrius jumped away as though he'd been electrocuted and then seemed to remember that we were still in the pitch black in a haunted house and crowded close again.

"Um, there are other people still waiting to come in," the actor said, and I grimaced at just how awkward he sounded. "You can't really do that in here…"

Demetrius audibly swallowed.

"Do you have night goggles?" he asked numbly.

"Uh, yeah, we all do," the guy said.

"Right. Well. I think we're done in here."

I bit my lip, reaching for Demetrius' hand, relief filling me when the other man didn't pull away but held on tightly.

"There's an escape door right here."

Light suddenly flooded over us as an exit door opened, leading into a small corridor.

"Thanks," I said, giving the young man a smile and hoping it wasn't too awkward. The guy smiled back and shut the door.

Finally, I was able to see Demetrius' face.

In the lights from the games nearby, flashing neon colors, I was disappointed, but not surprised, to see the familiar mask back in place, nothing visible beyond it.

"Demetrius—"

"Meechie," he said, eyes widening as his gaze fell on his son a few yards away.

Suddenly, we both noticed our hands were still clasped.

Demetrius yanked his away, a little harder than was necessary, to be honest.

He called his son's name, and Meech looked over, instantly disappointed to see his dad while he was trying to play games with his friends. And his disappointment only grew a moment later when Demetrius insisted it was time to go home.

Surprised, I nudged his arm, trying to get him to look at me for the first time since leaving the blackout house.

The moment he did, he looked away, cheeks darkening.

"We can stay a bit longer," I said. "He's having fun."

Demetrius just shook his head.

"No, we have to go now."

"Demetrius…"

I waited, hoping he'd look at me again.

"It's okay," I said softly when he didn't.

"Meech, come on," he snapped. "Say bye to your friends."

The ride home was a silent affair. Meech sat in the back, his arms crossed over his chest. Demetrius gazed somberly out the window.

When I pulled up outside their door, Meech barely waited

for the car to stop before he was out, stomping up the walkway.

Demetrius moved to do the same, but I reached out, catching him by the wrist.

"Demetrius," I said, and then, because I really had no other words for it, "it's okay. Really."

He blinked at me, swallowed, and then gently pulled his hand free.

"See you on Monday," he said.

I watched him until he disappeared behind his front door, locking me out, and then sighed, sinking heavily back into my seat.

I knew he didn't exactly seem ecstatic about our kiss, but I couldn't stop thinking about it.

The fun and excitement we had together, even the thrill of the haunted house had nothing on the way Demetrius' kiss had made me feel. I didn't think I would be able to be around him anymore without wanting those lips on mine again.

CHAPTER 11

DEMETRIUS

M‌IGUEL WAS MY SOMEBODY TO LEAN ON UNTIL I WENT AND DID *that*. Now everything had gone to shit. What the hell was wrong with me? What was I thinking?

No, that was the wrong question. What was *he* thinking? Kissing me, like that, in the dark with our adrenaline pumping.

Maybe it was just a mistake? In the darkness of that hellish blackout tent, maybe…

"Ah, shit." I couldn't even keep up that ridiculous train of thought as I signed off on my new car.

No grown-ass man accidentally kisses another grown-ass man. Unless he wanted to, and if that logic followed, I had to admit I wanted him to do it since I kissed him back.

I even moaned into his mouth.

Mortified couldn't even begin to explain how I felt. I was way too old to be questioning my sexuality. I couldn't remember a moment when I ever wanted to kiss another man. But I didn't just kiss a man, I made out with him. In public, of all places, with my son and his new friends right around the corner.

"Thank you," I murmured to the dealer, ignoring a barrage of text messages from Miguel.

Earlier in the morning, I sent him a message that I bought a new car and could get to and from work by myself from now on, which was true. It felt like a miracle when I opened my mailbox that morning to find my long-awaited insurance check waiting for me.

I thought I'd have to forgo every luxury to keep up the rideshares and cabs to avoid the inevitable. Or become a hermit. I even thought about buying an electric bike, if it meant not having to be stuck inside a small, confined, or concealed space with Miguel outside of work where Chris and Mike could keep us separated.

Thankfully, I didn't have to do anything other than get to the dealership, pay for my new Nissan outright, and keep it moving.

Literally and figuratively. At work, I had to practically jump through hoops not to get too close, the feeling of electricity racing across my skin every time we so much as brushed up against one another.

It was suffocating and unavoidable, which made it all the more unbearable. The site supervisor and the foreman couldn't exactly stop speaking during a build, and we had months to go on the project.

I couldn't let the professor down, but I didn't know how I was going to hold out for months with this burning desire to kiss him or run away eating me up inside.

Probably both, if I were honest with myself.

I hoped against reason that somehow we could just factory reset our relationship, like unplugging a TV and plugging it back in to "fix" a problem rather than dealing with the underlying issue head on.

I just had to keep all of our interaction about business and nothing else. Avoid his heavy gaze against my back, which also lingered on my body, and was undeniably tracing my lips.

All I had to do was slip into my car each day, do the bare minimum of talking, and lose myself in being Dad rather than whatever strange territory Miguel and I had crossed into.

So why am I about to drive to The Cantina for drinks after work?

Oh, right. I got it in my head to be more friendly with the crew when I thought working for Smithson Construction would become a long-term thing. Shot Mike and Chris a message after whatever that was at the pier went down.

I didn't want to go, but I also didn't want to back out last minute and solidify my unfriendly persona.

I'd even gone out of my way to arrange a sleepover at Meechie's friend's house so I could be free tonight. Quinten, thankfully, was his age on the same soccer team so they were probably having a blast. Kordell, his older brother, was going to watch them along with his foster sisters Ravi and Amanda. Their dad, Nate, had seemed like a great guy; I met him during one of Meechie's matches, and we hit it off.

Everything was going just right for once. But despite that fact, I needed things to not be working out so perfectly right now. Or else I had to finally man up and face the fact I made out with Miguel right in front of him.

I just couldn't see how things were going to end well if I went into that bar.

Fuck!

Clutching the steering wheel, I took as long as I could to parallel park on the street downtown. I probably should've caught a cab, but I promised myself I wouldn't get too drunk and do something I'd regret.

I threw one last Hail Mary, texting my son to see if he was having fun.

He'd been in a sour mood ever since I forced him to leave

Fright Night early. And I couldn't exactly be open and honest as to why.

I knew he was really happy to make friends, to go out tonight and hang out with someone other than me. But all he had to say was that he wanted to come home or he wasn't feeling well. Just something to give me a credible excuse to dip out.

But luck wasn't on my side tonight.

Meechie: I'm good!

Of all nights to become well adjusted to his new life in Gaynor Beach, it had to be this one. I sent a thumbs up back and got out of the car. There was nothing else I could do to waste any more time.

I waved stiffly as I entered the bar. Mike, Chris, and Miguel were already posted up, sipping on beers and chatting with the bartender. They all seemed rather friendly, and I figured that they were regulars here.

"Hey," I said, sitting down on a stool and ordering a drink.

I made a point to shoot Miguel a tight-lipped smile so we didn't seem too obvious as Chris slapped me on the shoulder and Mike raised his beer.

"Never thought we'd get you out here," Chris said.

"Same." Mike was laughing.

At me or at the situation? I could never really tell with them.

Miguel, on the other hand, just kept staring. It wasn't with the same intensity as he did at work, but I could tell he wanted to speak with me.

Preferably alone.

There was no way in hell that was happening.

I decided to order another beer, despite it tasting like lukewarm piss. Or, at least, what I assumed lukewarm piss would taste like. Again, I wasn't a big drinker.

But keeping my mouth occupied meant I didn't have to speak too much. A couple of beers couldn't hurt, right?

Wrong! About an hour in, I could already feel myself getting tipsy. I declined another drink so I could remain clear headed.

At first I was worried about sobbing over my ex. Now I was petrified that I would blurt out "what are we?" to Miguel in front of the guys.

I held my head in my hands, trying to drown out the football plays coming from the TV on top of Chris and Mike's laughter. It felt like the whole room was spinning.

"'Cuse me."

I didn't know if I needed to piss or just get up and stretch my legs, but I made a beeline for the bathroom regardless.

The inside was much posher than I expected, like the upscale ones you found in fancy burger joints with exposed rafter roofs and menus trying too hard to be different.

Most importantly, it was empty and quiet enough that I could be alone with my thoughts.

"Miguel?" I could feel him before I saw him, summoning the courage to look into the mirror over my shoulder.

Sure enough, it was him, closing the bathroom door behind him.

"We can share a cab if you want?"

Miguel was licking his lips as he stepped inside fully. Those weren't the first words I expected out of his mouth, but I guess it was better than coming straight out with what he really wanted to say to me.

I shook my head no, but the movement caused me to stumble backward, right into his arms.

Jerking away, I murmured, "No, it's fine. I'll call a cab. We're both too tipsy."

"I barely drank. My house's not far away. It's not a

problem for me to drop you off," he offered again. "Or I can call a cab. Whatever you want. A cab is probably better."

I was not about to risk being alone with Miguel for another minute. It wasn't that I didn't trust him not to jump my bones. I didn't trust my damn self.

Shaking my head *no* again, I tried to brush past him. But this time he didn't let me avoid him.

He reached out and grabbed my upper arm. Not too tight that I couldn't shrug it away, but firm enough that I stopped and turned to look at him.

"Can't we just... talk?"

About what, was what I wanted to add, but I kept my mouth shut. I didn't trust myself to speak anymore either. I just wanted out.

"I think...," I stammered, voice trailing off.

I swallowed hard and finished my sentence. "I think I should apologize."

"For what?" His eyebrows knitted in confusion.

Shifting to one foot, then the other, I whispered, "For kissing you back. I shouldn't have done that. I'm sorry. Let's just forget it ever happened."

There, I said it. Out loud. And I hoped it was enough for us to bury the memory like a frat story we never spoke of again after college.

But instead of reassuring me that it was nothing, Miguel moved towards me with confidence until I was pinned against a stall door.

His hand moved from my upper arm to my waist in a flash. But when I went to run away, his hands shot to my shoulders, bringing me closer, making me focus on him.

"What are you doing?" I murmured, his breath ghosting against me again.

I shuddered as he leaned even closer, whispering against my lips as I naturally leaned forward to kiss him back. "Are you sorry we kissed, or that it felt so good to give in?"

That was all he needed to say to smash through my last mental defense. Shutting my eyes, I closed the space left between us.

And this time, I didn't have enough adrenaline coursing through my body to blow it off as a mistake. Some nasty-tasting beer was coursing through my system, giving me liquid courage, yes, but I was far from drunk. I couldn't blame myself kissing him back this time on anything other than my desire for him now.

I clenched my fists, not sure where my hands should be as his tongue teased my bottom lip.

Miguel ran his large hands down my shoulders and arms as if he could read my mind, deepening the kiss, and this time moaning into my mouth.

The sound of him coming undone was turning me on. He tugged my wrists, and I wrapped my arms around his shoulders.

Miguel, in turn, clutched my ass, dragging my lower half against his body.

I groaned as his tongue sought mine, his taste and touch setting every nerve ending in my body on fire. I sighed, and he seized that moment to shove his tongue deeper down my throat.

He seemed to like kissing and had experience with more than one man by the way he was manhandling me. My lips felt clumsy against Miguel's, and my heart was pounding so hard I didn't know if I was having a panic attack or a heart attack.

Either way, there was no stopping this. As if I could deny my feelings for him for another moment while making out in yet another public place, because we couldn't seem to keep our hands off of each other.

Which I became keenly aware of when the doorknob started jiggling. I pushed Miguel away, but his reflexes were like lightning.

I could feel his heart thudding against my chest as he carefully shut the door to the stall behind us. He had us hidden away by the time whoever it was made it inside the bathroom.

They hadn't closed the door fully, probably a little drunk, allowing just enough sound from the bar to drift inside to mask our presence more. But if he so much as glanced downward, this guy was going to see too many feet in one stall.

"Shh," Miguel whispered against my ear as he worked my belt buckle.

The next thing I knew, his hand was dangerously close to my junk.

Oh no!

"What're you gonna do? Jerk me off with that guy standing out there?" I hissed into his ear as quietly as I could.

He seemed taken aback but then laughed so hard I could feel his stomach spasming against mine, burying his face into my neck to keep quiet.

"No," he whispered back. "I was trying to make it sound like we're not in here doing this. But if that's your kink, I'm never too old to try new things."

He seemed to think this situation was funny. I, on the other hand, was having a mental meltdown. I licked my dry lips, nervous, unsure of how to move this from the bathroom to any room other than this without getting caught.

And then I heard whoever it was stop by our stall, washing his hands.

Shit.

My nails dug into his broad back, dragging Miguel closer, out of fear or from surprise, I wasn't sure. I just wanted us to fold into each other and disappear altogether.

This guy was going to find us. Then what? The realization instantly snapped me back to reality, like a bucket of cold water splashed on my overheating brain.

But just as I was on the verge of outwardly freaking out,

Miguel took my chin into the palm of his hand, forcing me to look at him.

The crisp, sharp scent of sawdust and his natural, masculine scent filled my nose.

I could feel my cock stiffen, pitching a tent in my now too-tight pants. He pressed his leg in between mine, the pressure divine. I was about to lose it, to risk it all in some bar bathroom with some stranger a flimsy stall door away.

Relax, he mouthed to me, before going in for the kill.

The tip of his tongue teased my Adam's apple as he peppered kisses down my neck.

Strong, calloused hands that were undeniably masculine were all over me again. And yet, I was turned on. So painfully turned on and unable to move an inch as Miguel subjected me to his sweet, torturous embrace.

His hazel eyes clouded in lust traced every inch of me.

His hands, clutching my hips, dug into my skin.

His tongue and lips were relentless, threatening to swallow me whole.

And, most shockingly, his hard cock was smashed against my erection, and I loved it.

All of him was promising me what would come once we got out of here. It was incredible, and I knew it could be so much more if this asshole went away so we could get the fuck out of this bathroom!

For once, my prayers were answered.

The doorknob jiggled, and then the door opened and shut fully. The stranger was gone. The spell was broken, for now.

"Let's get out of here," I said as soon as I was sure he was gone.

We burst out of the stall, both of us fighting for air.

But as we separated, fixed our shirts, and walked out, I knew there was no going back now.

CHAPTER 12
MIGUEL

How I was supposed to act my usual self now was a mystery. To sit back, have a casual drink, chat with the boys, and joke with Evan, all the while ignoring what had just happened. Pretending I wasn't still in that washroom stall, still seeing Demetrius' heated gaze. That I wasn't right now *feeling* the phantom warmth of his body, the grip of his hands. That my cock wasn't aching from the tease it had been given by the one and only, hard-edged Demetrius Johnson giving himself over, possibly for the first time, to something he truly desired.

I felt like I'd touched a livewire; my entire body buzzed with electricity and static. I needed Demetrius to bring me back down—preferably after a long, hard session spread out on his back in my bed.

I bit my lip hard, glancing over at him. He was sitting back in his spot at the bar nursing that same drink he'd left unattended, pretending to listen to whatever Mike was enthusiastically describing. All because when we walked out, we realized we couldn't exactly run off together without it being noticed.

We had to at least finish our beers.

Chris was listening avidly, so Mike must have been telling an interesting story, but Demetrius and I had already checked out. There was no reason for us to be here anymore. There was no reason for false pretenses either.

I tipped back my last sip and pushed to my feet.

When I reached Demetrius, still planted on his stool, it was all I could do to not reach out and touch him.

He looked up at me like he half-expected me to jump him right out in the open this time.

"I'm going to head out," I said. "Want to share a cab?"

There. Nice and neutral. There was no reason for him to be mad. No one would question it. And he could easily say no...

"Yes."

My heart skipped in anticipation.

"What the hell... ?" Mike said slowly. "You're seriously *both* dipping already?"

They looked between us, and suddenly I seriously regretted my very public approach to this because there was suspicion in their eyes.

I didn't care. I had never hidden my sexuality from them, but Demetrius wasn't out. In fact, this was all very new to him. I didn't want him to freak out. Again.

I opened my mouth, some excuse on the tip of my tongue: I wasn't feeling well, I'd drank too much. They wouldn't buy either of those reasons, but luckily, Demetrius beat me to it.

"I told Miguel earlier that I had to leave before"—he looked at his phone—"yes, before eleven. My son has soccer practice first thing in the morning."

They seemed to accept that, but Mike gave me a look.

"Demetrius is a grown man, Miguel, he doesn't need you to escort him. Pretty sure he can handle a cab on his own without getting lost."

"Those fish tacos I had aren't sitting well with the whiskey." I shrugged.

They both grimaced and said goodbye. I had to hold back a sigh of relief until we were stepping outside the front door.

I would have grabbed onto Demetrius the moment the cold night air hit me. Shots still running through my blood even made me sway towards him, but he was standing off, a little bit too far, watching the streetlights, then the road, then the sidewalk.

I smiled watching him while he watched everything but me; then, letting instinct take over, I stepped right up to him.

He didn't back away the way I thought he would. Instead, a relieved sigh left him and his hands gripped the front of my shirt, keeping him steady.

He looked down the short inch to meet my gaze with a shaky breath.

Our lips brushed, and then he pulled back and swallowed.

"Is this about the fish tacos?" I asked.

He let out a surprised laugh.

"Demetrius," I said, trying not to laugh, tilting his chin so our gazes met again. "There were no fish tacos. I promise."

"No," he agreed, still chuckling. "I would have noticed."

Our lips brushed again. This time, I pulled back, turned, and approached the street. Demetrius was close behind me. If we were lucky, we'd catch a cab. Otherwise, we'd have to call.

I didn't want the hassle of waiting. I wanted to get home as quickly as possible.

It only took a minute of anxious waiting, of feeling Demetrius' heat next to me, of barely resisting giving up on getting anywhere and just kissing him senseless right in the open, before a cab turned onto the street.

I leaped out, waving them down triumphantly.

When it pulled over, I gripped Demetrius' hand, pulling him along after me, not willing to give him the chance to second guess this.

When we got in the cab, I told the driver my address and

nothing else. Demetrius didn't pipe up, didn't give his own as a second stop.

The small confirmation that he *wanted* to go home with me sent anticipation thrumming through me.

This was happening. Soon my hands would be on him.

Unable to help myself and desperate for another taste of what I would be getting, my palm slid over the smooth leather of the seat between us and didn't stop until it was draped over his thigh.

A little higher and I would feel him again, his generous erection that had briefly been against me, letting me know just how much I was affecting him.

Somehow, I managed not to scandalize him further by touching him where I wanted to. Instead, I teased myself by keeping my hand exactly where it was, even when he kept shifting and looking at me, my hand strong and hot on him, fingers gently rubbing his inner thigh.

I didn't know how we made it home, how we managed to pay and get out of the cab, but somehow, we ended up in front of my door.

Only as I stood there did I realize how long it had been. I couldn't remember the last time I'd had someone over. I couldn't even remember the last time one of my friends had been over. I always went to them. Maybe I didn't let people in as much as I thought I did.

Our gazes met as the key slid into the lock. His dark eyes were so warm and vulnerable. He was choosing to trust me and I wasn't going to let him regret it.

There would be no awkward conversations. I wouldn't put the kettle on or offer him something to eat. I wouldn't turn on the TV or show him around.

This was too big for any of that. Whether he wanted to acknowledge it or not, I could see it in his eyes.

And whether it was said or not, I knew what a risk this was for Demetrius, and I was honored to be given the chance.

That was why, the second the door was closed behind us, I didn't bother with the lights or taking off my jacket. I just turned, closing Demetrius into my arms and leaning into him, using our bodies to slam the door shut as he was pressed against it. Our lips clashed, missing slightly in the dark. His stubble scraped my cheek and my tooth caught his lip, but he shuddered and a desperate noise left him, and I knew without a shadow of a doubt how much he needed this— someone to completely let go with.

I wanted to whisper *you won't regret this*, but I knew any words would get him stuck in that big brain of his, and I didn't want him to think, just to feel.

CHAPTER 13

DEMETRIUS

A PART OF ME KNEW I WOULD REGRET THIS. THAT MIGUEL wasn't serious about me. We were friends progressing into that dangerous, murky territory of friends-with-benefits.

I knew without really confronting it that my feelings ran deeper than lust. But I was tired of holding back. Tired of pretending I wanted anything less than his mouth against mine and his hard cock pressed against me, every lingering touch and teasing kiss allowing me to fall deeper under his spell. To finally let go of all my doubts and worries and just *be*.

"Miguel..." His name was a sigh against his firm lips as we stumbled through the darkness, together, towards his bedroom.

He answered me by holding me closer. Miguel's firm, muscular arms were so foreign to me, yet they felt just right. His hands were under my shirt, then clutching my cheeks, his lips whispering sweet nothings in my ears along the way.

And then we were past his door, against the wall of his bedroom. The tips of my fingers ran through his silky hair with ease, and I relished the feeling, longing to touch him ever since that near miss at the pier. He slowed down, undoing my shirt buttons with surprising precision as his beautiful eyes captured mine and held.

They reminded me of the sunset, the moment my body knew that I wanted all of him.

I flinched, trying to process what was next as he tugged on my boxers. To the bed and then… I drew a blank. My mind couldn't really imagine it. I've never had sex with a man, hadn't ever dreamed of it let alone done the real thing.

And it was my first time. What if I messed up? My mind was starting to wander, worry, get sucked back into my usual neurosis.

As if to reassure me that everything was going to be okay, and that I just needed to let go and be in the moment, he held me close, bare chest to bare chest and whispered, "Relax."

And I did. His voice was like music to my ears, or more like medicine to a weary heart longing for more. Longing to let go.

I reached down, remembering to help him get undressed. My forehead rested on his as he pulled down my boxers. My dripping erection was already at the point of bursting. He fisted my cock without a word, stroking my aching shaft excruciatingly slowly.

My chest heaved as he focused on the head of my dick, so close that I could almost count his eyelashes in the dark. My toes curled into the carpet. I was so damn close after all that teasing back at the bar and that painful cab ride to his house where we were so close, yet too far.

He seemed obsessed with marking me, licking, sucking, and biting at my neck as I pumped my cock into his hand, my hips moving of their own accord. It was all too much, and my glasses were starting to fog over.

I felt so exposed, so raw, but it also felt all wrong. I wanted him to fuck me on his bed, not against the wall, so I could hold him close and pretend I never had to let him go.

"Wait," I whispered as he plucked my glasses from my face with his free hand.

He placed them on his nightstand, backing us closer to the bed, about to shove me down on it after I blew my load into his hand probably.

Miguel ignored my first protest, freeing his own cock as he moved my hand to grip his. It was heavy and thicker than I imagined and already leaking pre-cum. My hand sliding up and down trying to keep up with his pace. I was glad I couldn't see Miguel clearly now, only feel what his hand was doing to me, and me to him. Just enough cover to keep my brain working, albeit at a snail's pace.

"Wait, Miguel, please…"

Miguel peered at me, pulling away finally, his teeth scraping against my skin. I was going to have some huge, dark hickeys to hide by the morning.

"What's wrong?" he asked.

"I don't want this," I gasped, losing my breath as I stopped stroking, wrapping my hand around his so he would stop stroking me to death.

Devastated didn't begin to explain the look on his face. But I recovered quickly, not wanting him to get the wrong idea. That I didn't want him. I just didn't want him like this.

"Not you. I mean. *Fuck!* I don't want to come like this. I want to come with you inside me."

He was silent for so long that I was afraid I fucked everything up. And then he grabbed me with so much force he knocked the wind out of me.

"You don't know what you've done to me," he grunted as he turned around and forced me down on the bed. "But you're about to find out."

A delicious shiver snaked up my spine. I would've done this sooner, said something faster, if only I knew how good it would feel to let Miguel take control.

He was over me in an instant, pressing me down into his

sheets, which smelled just like him. To my dismay, he still stroked my cock. But this time he made it even worse, the tip of his tongue darting out, flicking against my nipple.

I jerked, surprised and turned on, trying not to think too hard about what was coming. His arm was my pillow, and his hand was firmly threaded through my hair, holding me in place. Forcing me to watch him make me come.

And I did, despite not wanting to, desperately trying to hold out for the real thing. Miguel bit my lower lip as I cried out, vicious white ropes of come staining his hand, my stomach, and the sheets as I orgasmed. My stomach spasmed, my whole body curling upward, before I flopped back down on the bed, exhausted from being pent up for over a week.

I lay there, a sticky hot mess, as he fumbled around above me. Next thing I knew, my lower half was propped up by a pillow, and his fingers were inside me, colder than before, but still covered in my own essence. It clicked why he did what he did, my muscles totally relaxed, but that faded away as my mind became a gentle buzz, replaced soon by absolute mindless bliss.

"Ugh," I grunted as he added a finger, and then another, until the pressure was just a little too much.

And then he went a step too far. I could feel his tongue between my balls, kneading the sensation skin between them and my hole. I jerked, slapping his shoulder.

Miguel chuckled, dragging himself up the bed. He made my worries disappear with a tender kiss and reminded me why he was in charge, clutching the nape of my neck, distracting me from what was going inside of me with his masterful tongue, as his fingers pulled out.

Finally, he pulled away. I was ready, I guessed. Ready as I'd ever be to take dick.

I bit down on my lower lip as he slid inside of me, inch after unforgiving inch. He held my legs apart at first, pressing down on my knees. But I couldn't hold the position, so he switched things up, gripping the top of my head as he pressed in deeper.

His cock was thicker, harder, and much deeper than his fingers too. I clawed his back, trying to close my legs. But all I succeeded in doing was dragging Miguel closer to me, and deeper still.

My eyes fluttered as he filled me to the hilt, balls nestled against me, my limp cock coming to life smashed between our stomachs. The hairs on my chest felt electrified as Miguel rocked against my waist, too deep. My mind went totally blank.

"You feel so good," Miguel was whimpering again, pulling out too slowly, so slow I could feel every twitch. "Too good."

He pulled out until only the head of his cock was still inside of me, then slammed back inside. I was breathless, his pace steady, heavy, brushing up against something I couldn't name inside of me. I reached for my shaft, pumping it, the pain and fullness giving way to another feeling, an earth-shattering high.

"Look at me," he murmured. "Look at me, Demetrius."

And I did, and it was too much. The look in his eyes was indescribable, something too close to love.

"Miguel!" I whimpered in between ragged breaths. "I'm going to come! You're going to make me come again…"

He captured my lips in a savage kiss, drilling me too hard, too deep, just right, so gently, until I no longer cared. The world was spinning, too hot, my body trembling as he dragged yet another orgasm out of me and a strangled scream.

Miguel's back tensed shortly after, his whole body stiff as Miguel buried his cock balls-deep one last time and came.

When he was finished, he didn't pull out, laying his full

weight on top of me, holding me close. And I knew not only was I going to regret this night, I knew then and there that I could never let Miguel go again.

CHAPTER 14

MIGUEL

I woke up on top of silky-smooth skin, my fingers stroking the light brush of hair across Demetrius' chest.

I was pressed up against his back, daddy spoon, morning wood pressed shamelessly between his perky cheeks.

I smiled, warmth and bubbling happiness threatening to float me away. I turned and pressed my lips to the nape of his neck, careful not to wake him as I slid lower.

Rolling him onto his back would probably wake him up, and I didn't mind awkward positions, so I straddled his long legs carefully.

One glance up at his peaceful face confirmed that he was sleeping. He looked so innocent, so sweet. So not like someone who had practically begged for my cock inside him last night.

His cock was thick and heavy, laying over his thigh and I bent low, gently dragging my lips over the soft skin.

Above me, Demetrius' breathing changed immediately, growing slightly shallower.

A long swipe of my tongue from tip to base made it hitch, and he shifted. I lifted quickly out of the way as he rolled onto his back, inadvertently giving me better access.

With a wicked smile I couldn't help, I lowered myself over his hips again and carefully sucked his hardening length into my mouth, all the way down.

The beauty of a cock that was still soft was that you could feel it growing in your mouth, filling with blood, lengthening, hardening, stretching. It was so erotic, so mouthwatering. I twisted my tongue around his length and suddenly, his hands were on my head, tangling into my hair, pushing me down to take it deeper while a strangled moan left him.

He was fully hard now and thrust up with loose, sleepy abandon, making me choke.

Immediately, his hands lifted off, and I pulled back, catching his sheepish expression.

"Sorry," he muttered breathlessly. "I didn't mean to."

The sight of Demetrius sprawled out in my bed first thing in the morning, looking sleepy and turned on, was a blessing.

I grinned.

"Don't be sorry. I wanted that reaction." I gripped his thick cock around the base and pressed my lips to the tip before going on. "I don't want you to hold back."

He shuddered and when I sucked his tip back into my mouth, watching him while I did, his jaw slackened, and his head fell back with a curse.

"Oh... Fuck," he murmured while I worked him.

It didn't take long before his hips pressed up, seeking more, tension running through his body as he came, hands tangled in my hair again.

I swallowed as best I could, but it had been a while since I'd sucked cock and it dripped from the corner of my mouth, down my chin before I could stop it.

Demetrius pulled me by the shoulders, and I tried to wipe it all off before our lips met, but he didn't seem to care. He moaned into my mouth, tongue delving deeper, tasting himself inside me and I would never, ever get enough of *this*

Demetrius. The one hungry for taste, sensation, and all the things he had been deprived of.

I kissed him back, just as fervently, my cock aching and leaking where it was sandwiched between us until he squeezed his hand in between and I lifted just enough to give him access. His grip was firm and confident, and he seemed to know that I liked it fast because he wasted no time stroking me, picking up the pace until I was gasping into his mouth, clutching his shoulders like a lifeline.

When I collapsed next to him, spent, ready to drop back off to sleep, he chuckled breathlessly.

I opened my eyes to find Demetrius' sweet smile, straight, white teeth, and honest, crinkled eyes. He shifted to face me and, for a while, we just smiled at each other.

My fingers traced the skin on the back of his hand. It seemed I was now unable to stop touching this man.

"You're not freaking out," I said.

His lips twitched, attempting to feign a frown.

"You expected a freak-out?" he asked.

"Oh yes," I agreed. "I thought getting you into my bed last night was a miracle, this morning would be a stretch, and you staying long enough for breakfast, a pipe dream."

He laughed.

"Who said I was staying for breakfast?"

I leaned in and kissed him, unable to resist.

The brush of lips lingered, neither of us wanting this to end just yet, but then Demetrius' stomach rumbled softly.

He pulled away, looking mortified enough that he may as well have farted unexpectedly.

"Aha, see? I knew you'd want to stay for breakfast."

He guffawed loudly, smacking me as I rolled away.

"Shower first?" I asked. "Or food?"

"Uh..." He lay in bed, looking up at me as I stood, clearly trying unsuccessfully to keep his eyes above neck level. His gaze dropped, cheeks darkening.

"How about you take a shower first while I cook?" I suggested.

His eyes snapped back up to meet mine.

"Yes. Okay."

I only managed to drag myself away, because Demetrius was looking a little self-conscious and if I stuck around, we wouldn't ever leave this bed.

I went to the kitchen and sorted through the fridge, glad I actually had some groceries.

The smell of fried eggs and toast filled the air while I waited for him. For the first time since I could remember, this house felt a little homier and more inviting. It was pretty bare in the decorations department, but it was filled with Demetrius and me and we were enough.

I was buzzing, foot tapping, whistling a happy tune. I was a cliché but didn't care. There was no way to suppress the excitement I felt.

Demetrius had *chosen* me to be the first man he ever made love to.

I couldn't hold back a smile while I plated our food, but Demetrius emerged, clean and tidy, back in his clothes from last night, frowning down at his phone, jacket slung over an arm.

"Sorry, looks like I can't stay for breakfast after all."

He looked up, saw me with two plates in my hands, and grimaced.

"Okay, maybe I can stay for a couple bites."

I set the plates at the table, glad he hadn't just run out the door, but the vibe was different. He was in a rush, not really looking at me while he scarfed down his food.

"Is it Meech?" I asked.

He nodded.

"He wants to be picked up. It is getting late."

I nodded.

"Of course."

Getting annoyed over a dad putting his son first would have been stupid, but I couldn't help feeling a little disappointed that we weren't able to spend more time together today, just the two of us holed up in my house.

He swallowed down his last bite of toast, chased it with a gulp of coffee, and was on his feet.

"Okay, thanks for everything," he said in the same tone he thanked me for rides, like it wasn't a big deal.

Before he could literally run from my house, it occurred to me that he might not know that this was more than a hook-up for me.

I was on my feet and at his back before he finished pulling on his shoes. When he straightened, I pulled him into an embrace, his tense back to my chest.

I kissed his neck, and he sagged against me slightly.

For once, I wasn't sure what to say. To gush about how big this had felt to me would be too much. To thank him would only add to the misconception that I only wanted him for sex.

"This was... nice," Demetrius said quietly, beating me to it.

I rested my chin on his shoulder and nodded.

"That's an understatement" was all I said and that seemed to be enough.

He wiggled around to face me and kissed me, softly and quickly.

"I'll see you on Monday," he said.

"I can't wait."

He chuckled and left, gaze lingering even as he was shutting the door.

I let out a soft groan and rested my head against the door.

That shy smile of his was going to kill me and I really *couldn't* wait to see it again.

In fact, I only made it a couple hours before texting Demetrius. Because I was a jerk, I sent only a photo of my rumpled bed sheets, grinning while I imagined the expression he would make upon seeing the picture. I would bet he would try to hide his phone in shock, even if no one else was around.

To my surprise, he played along. It was only a minute later that I got a response: the emoji of a thinking face wearing a monocle, followed by *"Did your mother never teach you to make the bed?"*

I laughed and spent the next few minutes changing the sheets.

I took another picture and sent it over with a winky face. *There, all ready for someone to come mess it up with me again.*

Demetrius laughed at the message. Really, I was surprised at how well he was taking this.

I had wanted him to loosen up. I'd wanted to get him to relax a little, to be himself. I hadn't expected it to happen so quickly though. This was good. He was more willing to play along than I'd first thought and that was a good thing, because for the first time since the crash and burn of my relationship with Rodrigo, I thought maybe I could trust someone again.

Demetrius wasn't the type to cheat or run around behind my back or pretend to like me more than he did. No, quite the opposite. He had pretended to like me *less* than he did. Now I knew though and there was no going back.

It was such a shame that he had a new car now. That meant I had to wait an extra twenty minutes before seeing him, and then, when I did, he was already chatting to Chris about the day's plans and I couldn't just walk up to him and kiss him the way I wanted to. I didn't think he'd appreciate that though.

All I got was a "hey Miguel," and then he was back to work talk, including me in it this time.

Disgruntled, I used the excuse of reading over his shoulder to come up close behind him. The overpowering smells of drywall dust and PL glue and fresh cut wood mingled with his cologne, but it was still heavenly. Something about the way Demetrius smelled was calming and nostalgic and homey. I just wanted to bury my face in his neck and hug him all day and maybe I was standing a little too close because Demetrius shifted away, giving me more room to look at the plans.

I wanted to talk to him, see how he was, but Chris started talking about the weekend, about how a fight broke out in the bar after we left and Mike had gotten an accidental elbow in the face from trying to pull the guys apart.

Despite myself, I was drawn into the story. Then Mike arrived with fresh stitches on his forehead and launched into the story from his side.

By the time they were done talking about it, it was already past first break. Demetrius emerged only to make a coffee run, picking one up for each of us. He stood with us on the porch for a few minutes while we chatted. Only once did I catch his eyes on me and he looked away just as quickly.

I understood. I didn't want to out him when he wasn't ready either, and we weren't even in a relationship properly, were we? Still, it was driving me crazy not to be able to reach out and touch him, to smile at him and talk to him and ask how Meech was and if he was ever going to tell him that his friend Miguel was more than a friend now—I was seriously getting ahead of myself. But I couldn't stop.

By the time lunch came around, I was over pretending I didn't want to see Demetrius. I didn't give the guys a reason; I didn't *need* a reason to go talk to my site supervisor. I was supposed to be the foreman, after all. We were supposed to chat and have meetings.

When I reached his door, Demetrius was talking to the plumber on the phone. I could hear his disgruntled voice.

"You can't come until the twenty-fifth?" he demanded incredulously. "We need those toilets placed before then."

I knocked gently and opened the door, peeking in.

Demetrius waved me in, and I sat back in the chair opposite his desk, waiting.

Apparently I was a distraction though, because Demetrius' gaze finally fixed on me. We watched each other.

"Uh-huh," he muttered into the phone. "Um. I'll call you back."

He hung up without waiting for a response.

"Scheduling issues?" I asked.

"Huh? Oh, yeah."

He looked down, shuffling papers around aimlessly.

"I've been dying to kiss you all day," I blurted.

Demetrius stopped what he was doing, fixing me with a relieved smile.

"Yeah?"

"Definitely."

"Me too," he admitted, and there was that same damn smile, the shy one that drove me crazy.

"Well, hell, what are we waiting for?"

I made a dramatic show of shoving things on the table out of the way. Demetrius was laughing by the time I pressed my lips to his and I was smiling too, heart soaring with gratitude at the feel of his lips on mine. Kissing him was addictive, and I didn't want or need to stop.

I pulled back, groaning.

"Over the table was the worst possible way to get to you."

I straightened and walked around it this time while Demetrius swiveled to face me.

Gripping both arms of his chair, I leaned down, kissing him again, deeper this time.

A soft moan left him and his head tilted back, giving me better access, and I found myself slipping lower, kissing his jaw and neck, gently biting his collarbone.

Reaching down, I gripped him by the knees, spreading his legs apart, and then lowering between them.

"Can I suck you off again?" I asked.

"Right now?" He looked conflicted. His gaze flickered to the door.

"I'm the only one who ever comes in here," I reminded him.

Biting his lip, Demetrius quickly reached down, pulling his belt open and undoing his pants. He lifted his hips, shoving them down until I grabbed on and pulled them all the way to the ankles.

He was already hard, cock straining towards me.

I took my time stroking and licking him before sucking him down, all the way. I pretended that we weren't on a lunch break, that we had limitless time simply because I wanted to savor this. I loved the way he moved, the small twitches, the way his breath hitched, the way he gripped my shoulders when he was going to come.

This time, when his body started to shudder with his release, I swallowed it all down. Didn't want to make a mess in his neat office.

The second his cock stopped flexing in my mouth, he pushed me back. I wiped my lips, ready to ask him what was wrong.

"Stand up," he ordered, voice still breathy.

As soon as I was on my feet, he pushed me back until I was leaning against the desk. Only when he reached for the button on my thick work pants did I realize what he was going to do.

I helped him push them down, out of the way along with my boxers, and then he stared at my erection, hard as a rock and already leaking.

Carefully, he leaned closer and gently licked the tip, tasting it.

I took a shuddering breath, fingers gripping the desk's edge to ground me. I didn't have to ask to know that this was his first time trying this; he'd basically told me as much. I wanted him to take his time experiencing it. That meant not immediately coming on his face the second he started.

I had to bite my lip and shut my eyes as his lips closed around me.

"Fuck," I groaned.

When he started to bob gently, saliva slicking me, his hot mouth stroking my length, I cursed again and gripped his shoulders.

"That's so good, Demetrius. I'm not going to last long," I warned.

He seemed to take that as encouragement, lips tightening and sucking me harder. My hips thrust forward of their own accord, and he gagged as my tip pressed into the back of his throat, choking him a little.

"Sorry," he mumbled.

I wanted to say it was my fault, but he gripped me suddenly in a firm hand and slipped his lips around my cock, and I made the mistake of watching him do it this time and that was all it took. My whole body shuddered with the strength of my orgasm. I had to push Demetrius back, trying to get him off of me before I *really* choked him, but I was already coming, and it splashed across his chin.

He didn't seem to care, opening his mouth and letting the last spurts land across his tongue before licking the sensitive skin again as it started to soften.

It seemed to take forever for me to come back down to earth.

With trembling fingers, I pulled my pants back up and reached into the pocket for the clean rag inside.

"What's this?" Demetrius asked, taking it.

"For your—"

I waved at the mess still on his face.

He didn't remark on the fact that I'd given him the torn remnants of an old shirt that was covered in oil stains from work, he just used it to wipe his face down.

"Better?" he asked.

I nodded and watched while he stood to pull his pants back up, then, because I couldn't help myself, I reached for his chin, turning him to face me. I kissed him again, relishing the way his arms came around me, the way our tastes mingled.

"You gave me a blowjob," I suddenly said in awe.

He groaned, pushing me away.

"I know. I was there."

I laughed and grabbed onto him, not letting him push me any further away.

"It was good." I kissed him again. "You sure that was your first one?"

His cheeks darkened and he nodded.

"You should get back to work before anyone notices how long you've been gone."

"It's lunchtime."

He rolled his eyes.

"Okay, get back to lunch then."

"Come with me."

"I can't," he argued. "It'll be too obvious."

My brows rose.

"Yeah?"

Without smiling this time, he looked me straight in the eyes.

"I won't be able to hide it."

My heart gave an unnatural flip. For a moment, I didn't know what to say. Then he pressed his lips to mine, that same quick, chaste way he had at my door, and he turned around, giving a gentle push.

"Go. I have things to do."

Chuckling, I followed his orders.

As the day went on, I realized he was so right.

I couldn't stop smiling.

"Can you believe this beautiful day?" I said for the fourth

time when I caught Chris staring at me suspiciously again. He and Mike just shook their heads at me and carried on.

Then, when I saw Demetrius circling the site, measuring, and talking on the phone to one of the trades, it was all I could do to keep working. And whenever he caught my eye, he always looked away with that same sweet smile that made my stomach erupt with butterflies.

One thing was for sure: Demetrius had to come out fast because we weren't going to be able to hide this for long and I wasn't going anywhere.

CHAPTER 15

DEMETRIUS

SOME DAYS, I LONGED FOR THE TIME MIGUEL WAS A NUISANCE and not my lover. If only because we couldn't keep our hands to ourselves any longer. Cuddling behind walls and sneaking kisses when the guys weren't looking. Giggling like kids over little things. Sneaking off together whenever we had some free time.

We were having a full-blown fling. And I was loving every second of it.

Chris gave me a strange look as I walked past. We had to install the new staircase from the kitchen into the basement today, after finally getting the proper permits to do so. Which was crucial because the basement was effectively becoming an apartment for Hiroshi's daughter and grandsons.

It took me a while to realize why he was staring, that I was whistling, yes, *whistling* on the job. Like Miguel did in the morning, visibly giddy. I straightened up instantly.

"Everything good?" I asked, squaring my shoulders.

Ever since that night at the bar, I couldn't help but think Mike and Chris were on to us. And it was stressing me out. I was most likely reading too much into things, as usual, but there was something more than curiosity in their eyes when they looked at me now. Almost like they were amused.

"Yup, all good," Chris said, eyes pinching in the corners as he dragged a hand through his brown hair.

"Are you heading out for lunch?" Mike asked, mustache lifting up in the corners, steel gray eyes twinkling.

"With Miguel," Chris added with a smirk. "I thought your car was fixed?"

I froze, racking my mind for something that didn't sound like an excuse.

"Ah, yeah. As a thanks for driving me around all that time. Do you guys want to come? Bring you something back?"

They looked at each other and shrugged.

"We're good here, boss," Chris said, this time smiling as he and Mike grabbed their lunches and headed out back.

I nodded, happy they didn't invite themselves along. Because I was trying to do something more than eat lunch with Miguel.

I licked my lips, middle finger teasing them as I grabbed my chin. Remembering the taste of his cock rammed down my throat, the absolute thrill of knowing anyone could walk through that door and see us. All the near misses since then.

...*Maybe I am developing a kink?*

Whatever the case, I wasn't planning anything sexual today. I wanted to try something out, a little more low key, hopefully intimate in a different way.

Sneaking out during work hours was no better than fooling around on the job, but at least today we wouldn't be making out in almost plain sight of our co-workers. Or taking suspiciously long breaks in my studio.

And I wanted to try something... date-adjacent. It felt like all we were doing was kissing, cuddling, and fucking. Because we were. And while Miguel seemed happy with the arrangement, I was hoping we could mold things, turn towards something more.

Slowly, as Alonso had drilled into my mind. While he was the only gay guy I knew personally, besides Miguel, I wasn't brave enough to send him a message that I was sleeping with a man online. But I had worked up the courage to ask the single dad group how to get back out there, and if they had been in a similar situation as me, keeping the gender vague.

And Alonso had, surprisingly, with his boyfriend. And he insisted that I take things slow, not rush into getting into another relationship. I should be having fun, not diving head first back into serious commitment.

Which I appreciated, but maybe I was just hard headed. Things felt good between us, great even, but also uneasy. I wanted us to be a little more committed to each other, instead of doing all the things you did when you dated, without the official title.

I flinched as hands encircled my waist. "Miguel!"

"Hmmm," he murmured, chin on my shoulder, hugging me from behind, holding me close.

As much as I wanted to melt into his embrace, I struggled away. I wasn't going to let myself get distracted today.

"You ready?" I asked, adjusting my glasses.

"Yes, lead the way." He sounded bemused at my attempt to be the guide for once.

I had to ask a lot of roundabout questions to finally find a place to eat, or at least grab a snack, somewhere that Miguel hadn't already been to. It seemed as though he was Gaynor Beach's number one ambassador, having seen and done just about everything. Aside from visiting this nearby bakery.

We took my car down to Gaynor Village, which wasn't far from the job as it was the heart of town. We passed Meechie's school, including the middle school and high school. And finally we made it to a block full of smaller shops. I could smell the aroma of freshly baked goods and sweets as soon as we parked and stepped up to Nice Buns.

"They're supposed to be really good," I said as I went to walk inside. "We can grab something to go and then eat our real lunches at the pier, if you want?"

"Nice buns at Nice Buns? I'm in," Miguel said while nodding his head.

I tilted my head at him, confused. "Yes, Nice Buns. That's the name of the store."

"No, I'm looking at them." He pinched my side to make it known he wasn't talking about the bakery.

I doubled back, laughing. He didn't skip a beat when it came to flirting.

I grumbled to quit it underneath my breath, though I was still cheesing all the same. Miguel was a big, obnoxious flirt. But I played along most of the time because it felt good to be wanted. To be with him.

But he was also reckless and careless about the fact that we were in the middle of the street. I dragged him inside before he could slap my ass or something else embarrassing.

We dipped in and out quickly, and as I suspected he would, he got something loaded down in sugar. Glazed, sprinkled, and probably creme filled. The sight of Miguel happily munching on his donut was making my stomach flip if I were honest. I wasn't that big into sweets, and he most definitely had a sweet tooth.

I opted for some glazed munchkins, not wanting to ruin my appetite. And I hadn't found much time to work out recently, so I didn't want to overeat.

One thing I used to be very religious about was exercising in the evening. But now that my nights were crammed full with helping Meechie or putting out flames at Winchelsea House, I didn't have much time for myself.

Besides moments like these. We got to the pier in no time and took a seat where we had before. I still hadn't seen one of those beautiful sunrises yet, but the evening breeze and tie-dye skyline never disappointed.

"Here." I handed Miguel his real lunch.

I wasn't a chef or anything, but it felt good to give back, provide in my own small way. And he seemed to like them.

We ate in silence, watching the waves and the occasional beach-goer. Fall was finally starting to feel a bit chilly in Gaynor, and I started second-guessing if we should've eaten at the bakery instead.

"You know, I really want to take y'all to the lighthouse at some point. Maybe have a picnic, when it's warmer."

"Meechie and me?" I asked, like that wasn't the case.

"Don't I always? You and Meech are a package deal, after all."

I nodded. Butterflies. Another date beforehand would be good though, right? Not that this was a date, officially, but it was one of the few times we weren't doing something alongside my son or with me on my knees.

Miguel leaned into me, resting his head on my shoulder. I tried to play coy, like it wasn't affecting me, but what I wouldn't give to be able to lean over and kiss him.

I guess I could have. The pier was emptier than it most likely would be in the summer. But there were still too many people around. I opted instead to hold his hand, dragging it into my lap. Even that felt a little too risky.

Miguel grinned, approving, but then he was leaning too close again, about to kiss me. I turned my face away at the last moment.

Miguel was a little too into PDA, and unfortunately, I was finding out the hard way.

He sat up suddenly, clearing his throat as he looked me over.

"We need to get back to work," I said, though I didn't want to leave just yet. But we had to. For once, I didn't want us to end up having sex. Oakdale was too close, which meant temptation was too.

He blinked, a little surprised. "We're going to go back? Already? I'm sure I can buy us some time…"

He trailed off, squinting with a lazy grin. I'm sure he could have bought us some time, but then this whole not-a-date-date would've been for nothing. We'd be back at square one.

Casting a quick glance around and seeing no one too close, I gave him a chaste kiss and pulled away.

"Yes, let's go back now. This was nice, wasn't it?"

I tugged him up and parted, walking side by side before he closed the distance between us. And I was very thankful 'cause Miguel was like an oven, warming me against the now-biting cold.

"It's always nice to unwind with you."

We smiled at each other. And I waited, and waited for him to say something more. To my disappointment, he didn't, but I figured that would come in time. It would probably be perceived as me being pushy to say anything else. One donut and a promised picnic wasn't the end all be all of dating. I'd find the perfect time to say the right words to take us to the next level.

Walking back to my car, shoulder to shoulder, we chatted about anything that came to our minds. But a little tendril of doubt weaved its way into my mind, that maybe I was fundamentally misunderstanding our relationship, and what we were building towards.

That was, if we were building towards anything at all.

But I decided to not dwell on that thought too much. We had time to cross our t's and dot our i's later. For now, we were just having fun.

Right?

The ride back to work felt like a breath of fresh air, and I was feeling thankful to Alonso for the advice. To take things slow, and not blurt out declarations of love when it had only been a month. Though it felt like we'd been together much longer than that already.

I was floating on cloud nine, about to be whistling my joy again, maybe even skip across the construction zone. Until we made it back, that was. And I saw what happened.

"What's going on?" I asked as Miguel and I came inside, Mike and Chris's faces rigid.

"Ah… Just take a look," Chris finally managed.

I walked over stiffly towards the new kitchen stairs leading to the basement. Pulling out my measuring tape, I confirmed what was already obvious to see by the time I walked down them. Too much cement had caused the steps to settle all wrong. Somehow, I had miscalculated the landing floor height and the boys poured too much concrete. The stair height was not up to code with the landing.

Seeing as the floor was too high, there was no way we could accommodate the full step needed to try and salvage the steps. We would have to dig out a new landing and pour a new foundation for that area. And it would take an engineer to help us fix this. It wasn't something small, not at all. And it was already a pain in the ass to schedule contractors as it stood.

I knew the look on my face wasn't good by the audible gulping I heard as I ascended the stairwell.

Miguel spoke first. "What's the damage?"

"There's no way this staircase will pass inspection. We gotta fix it."

Miguel nodded, and Chris and Mike went out, probably to get some tools. But Miguel didn't seem overly worried. And I couldn't believe how nonchalant he was acting.

"We'll get it done, don't worry."

"That's it? You…" I pursed my lips, shooting a quick glance at where the guys had left. "You know this got fucked up while we were upstairs."

He grimaced. I hoped I got my point across without going into detail. But he shook his head and shrugged. Like it was nothing.

"We made a mistake," Miguel began. "It happens! We'll order a new batch of cement and get to work. Don't worry about it. It's not going to blow the budget. We have more than enough time and money to fix it."

He reached for me and I stepped back unconsciously, taken aback by his reaction. Of course, I didn't expect him to freak out. Mistakes happened on the job all the time, even with the best of plans and intentions. But we both knew this wasn't that. I had been absent minded, too busy worrying about sucking his dick rather than making sure things were perfect downstairs.

I wanted to explain myself, about how important this project was to me *and* the professor. That he wasn't just some faceless rich client with enough budget to make it work. That this would cause Mike and Chris and Miguel extra labor when we could've avoided it if we just gotten it right the first time.

But that shouldn't have mattered. I shouldn't have needed to explain the obvious. We should be delivering our best, always. And Miguel and I both knew this mistake happened because we were too busy fucking around—literally.

Shaking my head, I said, "Fine. Let's just get back to work."

There was no point in arguing. Like Miguel said, it would get fixed, eventually. But I couldn't stop the nagging voice in the back of my mind warning me to pump the brakes. It was one thing to have a fling with a co-worker. It was another to let it botch projects we were working on.

Especially when he didn't seem to care about me on a deeper level anyway, despite me trying to read too much into every lingering glance and touch we shared.

CHAPTER 16

MIGUEL

I STARED AT THE TEXT THAT I'D GOTTEN THIS MORNING.

Sorry, phone was charging. Didn't see your message.

It was a classic excuse not to get back to someone in my opinion, partially because it was usually true, but I knew that wasn't the case with Demetrius. I'd texted him at *five* to ask if he and Meech wanted to do something. I'd been promising them a picnic by the lighthouse before the weather got too cold. He'd blown me off.

That, coupled with the last two days... the way he was suddenly too busy to get caught alone with me. The way he avoided eye contact.

It was hard to wrap my head around. Mistakes happened on jobs. That was part of the territory. We were only human. You couldn't be at one hundred percent all the time. When the new order of concrete arrived on Monday, we'd sort it all out and everything would be fine. Yeah, there was more work involved, but so what? This was an expensive reno. There was room for that in the budget.

Was that really the whole reason he was distancing himself from me?

I trudged up the stairs to Winchelsea House feeling something like dread at the thought of seeing Demetrius. I wanted to fix things, to go back to that happy stage we'd been in a few days ago. Things were too new to go haywire so fast.

"Jesus, what's wrong with you?" Mike asked. "You okay?"

It wasn't like my gruff carpenter friend to catch on to emotions, so when I glanced up and saw the curious look in his eyes as he set up the chop saw for the day, I knew I was leaking my feelings a little too much.

I shook myself and forced a smile.

"I'm good, just tired."

He seemed to buy it, and I managed to keep a smile going until I was nailing in the board and batten pieces into the kitchen wall. We were each doing different areas, and no one was watching me so, as often happened when doing repetitive work, my thoughts wandered.

I just couldn't understand what Demetrius was so upset about. Fooling around at work wasn't such a big deal. We only did it on breaks. Maybe it would be frowned upon, but we were both adults. We could at least talk about it, and move things home after hours if that was what he wanted. If he would talk to me, of course.

"Miguel, can I see you for a minute?"

I nearly jumped out of my skin at the sound of Demetrius' voice.

He was leaning against the door jamb, watching me with knowing eyes.

Probably because I hadn't responded to his message this morning and even Mike could tell I was depressed.

I stood and followed Demetrius into the hall where we wouldn't be seen. I had to cross my arms to stop myself from touching him.

"What's up?" I asked.

He turned, looked me over, and bit his lip.

"Are you okay?" he asked. "You look upset."

"Yeah, just, you know…" I sighed. "You blanked me."

His cheeks darkened and he shifted.

"Sorry," he muttered. "My phone died…"

So, he was sticking to that.

My gaze landed on the floor. It was next on the list after the basement was fixed. A beautiful charred wood would fill the entire ground floor. I wasn't looking forward to being on my hands and knees for weeks on end. My back ached at the thought of it.

"Do you want to come to see Meechie's soccer game with me tonight?" Demetrius suddenly asked. "It's his first one in Gaynor Beach."

I looked up, surprised.

"I went to a couple of their practices. The team is good. It'll be fun."

A smile pulled at my lips.

"I'll take any excuse I can to cheer that kid on," I said.

A genuine smile overtook Demetrius' face. He touched my arm, still folded.

"That means a lot, thank you," he said gently. "He'll be happy you're there."

I guessed from the way Demetrius looked at me that *he* would be happy too. When I dropped my arms and reached for him though, he barely let me touch his hand for more than a second before he was pulling away.

"I have to make some calls," he said.

I nodded, watching him ascend the steps, never looking back at me.

I felt cold for the rest of the day, even after my body was heated from work. Meeting Demetrius at the field later that day and being greeted with only a wave made it worse.

When I sat next to him, I could feel the way he shifted away and the tension, the awareness of me next to him, like he was ready to move even further if I tried to touch him.

Somehow, I managed to cheer Meech on, finding some enjoyment in the fact that he was having fun. I might have hollered the loudest when their team scored, and when his sweet face turned and waved at me and Demetrius in the crowds, that helped a little, but not enough.

Especially when I sat back, accidentally bumping Demetrius' shoulder, causing the other man to shift nearly half a foot away, his lips pursed.

I had to take a deep breath and school my features before I could say anything. I managed to keep my gaze on the kids and avoid glaring at him.

"I'm not contagious," I finally said, and then, I really couldn't help fixing him with an unimpressed look. "You're not going to catch something from me... in fact, I kind of thought that you *liked* getting touched by me."

Demetrius glanced furtively around. No one was close enough to hear my whispered words, but he still checked twice.

"It's not that," Demetrius eventually whispered back. "I'm just not ready to advertise this."

I tried to remember what that had been like. It was so long ago that I'd embraced my sexuality. I was ten years older than Demetrius, not to mention I had figured it out a lot younger. As in, I was pretty sure I was thirteen the first time I checked out a guy's ass. That was, what, twenty-six years ago? Then, I'd still mostly dated girls until Rodrigo, and I'd met him in my twenties. By then, I'd had no fucks to give over the opinions of others. But that was me and my personality. I'd never really cared about pleasing others. Demetrius, on the other hand, had a whole world to conform to. Not to mention a son that had an image of him as the straight-laced father. He hadn't grown up traveling the world the way I had, where the people you met were only a flash in the pan, gone the next day. His people had stayed. Even the ex had tried to make it last; why else would she have gotten married at such a young age?

I sighed.

"You're so damn responsible."

Demetrius frowned at me. I looked at him and met those lovely dark eyes, so full of emotion. I couldn't even manage to be mad.

Instead, I shrugged, giving in.

"I like you," I said. "You know, everything doesn't always have to be so… *heavy*. Just relax."

A cheer erupted and I looked over, just in time to catch the tail end of Meech's team scoring a goal. He looked over at us and I could see his bright smile from where we sat.

I clapped loudly, feeling a bit guilty for missing it and turned my full focus to the game.

CHAPTER 17

DEMETRIUS

Everything doesn't have to be so heavy? I marched across the parking lot, leaving Miguel to go to his own car. I didn't look back, more pissed off than I really should have been.

I shoved my son's extra duffel bag to the side in the trunk of my car, to make room for more gear. But my mind was far away, unable to really find joy in the fact that they won and he looked so happy about it, too, when they hoisted up their trophy.

I wanted to make some kind of witty comeback to Miguel during the rest of the game, but I opted for silence instead. Not because I wanted to leave him in the dark as to what I was thinking, but the fact I was genuinely shocked took my words away.

All I could manage once the game was over was that I'd call him. Then I cheered and snapped a picture of Meechie's team, sent it to Denise and my family group chat, and then I left to wait for Meechie by the car as we planned.

Miguel probably didn't mean much by his comments. That I was too responsible. That I was making things heavy by not being more affectionate.

At least, that was how I interpreted what he'd said.

But it didn't hurt any less. If anything, I thought I was doing both of us a favor. Keeping things light and airy, friendly on the outside, steamy behind closed doors.

So why was he boxing me in, accusing me of treating him like some disease? For fuck's sake, I was giving him blowjobs in my office! I was so hands on with him at work we'd completely botched the installation of the basement stairs.

How much more "affectionate" could I be?

I scanned the parking lot, as families from the home and away teams loaded up in cars. My son and the kid he'd befriended and had a sleepover with were nowhere in sight. I'd promised to drop them off, but they were probably still in the locker room changing.

Then I froze, feeling a presence at the nape of my neck.

For what felt like the first time, Miguel saw me before I noticed him. His eyes were already on me when I looked up, his hand reaching into his back pocket for his keys. He stopped, making a beeline in my direction.

I didn't want any drama in front of all these people, seeing as there was a good chance most of them either attended Meech's school or had a kid there.

Steeling my nerves, all I could think about was how could he not understand why I was trying to be more careful?

Miguel was… out? Was that the right word for it? Openly bi or gay was what I settled on in my mind.

But *I* wasn't. Hell, I still couldn't really wrap my mind around the fact that I was attracted to him. And trust and believe I tried to test out if I had some hidden attraction to men.

Maybe I had just found the wrong kind of porn, but it seemed Miguel was the only one doing it for me for now.

He was my first, and we weren't in a relationship.

A situationship, at best, fuck buddies at worse. But not a relationship.

He said he liked me, which made my heart squeeze at

first. But liking me and loving me were two very different things.

And our sex life was already leaking all over our professional lives. Did it have to spill out on the benches of Meech's soccer match too? While we still figured things out?

What was so wrong about keeping things on the down low while we were having fun? Loosening up, as he liked to say. Or that word I was starting to hate, learning to *relax*.

He was the one making things heavy, not me.

"Demetrius," he said as he reached my side, stopping a few inches away from my face, my back against the closed trunk door.

Miguel looked hurt, like he had all day, and I felt my resolve waver.

Why were things so hard already? Shouldn't we still be in the puppy love phase still? Puppy lust? Whatever, just not fighting.

Not that I would really know. My one and only relationship began in high school and ended last year, so maybe I was working off a faulty notion of how things worked normally.

"Can we talk about this later, please," I whispered between clenched teeth as gently as I could. "I don't want to argue. I don't want to fight."

Any more teeth clenching, and I'd have to tack on a dentist bill to my running expenses.

"We're not arguing," he insisted, despite everything in his body language to his tone screaming the opposite.

Please be for real!

I didn't say it out loud, lest I escalate things further, but I wanted to. We were arguing. It was obvious by the way some people shot us lingering looks.

"Let's talk later…"

"Why can't we talk right now?" he demanded.

Why is he being so direct all of a sudden?

"Are you sure we should? It feels like we're arguing."

"We're not." This time I could hear the anger in his voice.

I resisted the urge to roll my eyes. If he could be serious for one damn minute. Pretending we weren't arguing didn't magically make this *not* an argument.

I hated fighting. Hated misunderstandings. Detested going to bed mad at someone...

Someone I liked a lot. It was way too early to even *be* fighting.

"Okay." My tone was flat, noncommittal. I just wanted whatever this was to be over.

He groaned, nearly ripping his hair from his scalp by how hard he brushed his hair.

I was starting to feel boxed in by his presence, shooting desperate glances over his shoulder. But Meech wasn't running up to my rescue anytime soon.

How did things take such a hard, sharp turn for the worse?

I didn't want to apologize. What had I done wrong? But I felt I needed to, even if I didn't want to. Anything to avoid this... *tension* that was making me feel sick.

"I'm sorry, okay. I'm sorry and we'll talk later and I'll stop... overthinking."

There, that should do it.

But to my dismay, that seemed to make Miguel even more... worried. Hurt? Confused?

Maybe all three.

"Why are you apologizing? Do you even know?"

"Of course I do. You... No, *I* have been avoiding too much PDA. I get it. I just didn't appreciate what you said, was all. But I get it! I won't avoid you. I didn't think I was being that obvious, okay."

"What?"

"Saying I was making things heavy."

"I never said that! I said everything doesn't have to be so

heavy for *you*. You're always stuck in that big head of yours. You're always overthinking things."

I squinted, not knowing if I should laugh because he said I had a big head or overthink some more.

"What do you want?" He reached for me, tugging on my fingertips. "It's a simple question. I'm not asking you to propose, Demetrius. *Relax*."

This time I couldn't stop myself from rolling my eyes.

"I'm trying, but you're going to give me a heart attack if you try to kiss me in the parking lot of my son's school. Let's make up somewhere more private, hm?"

"Who said I was trying to kiss you?" Miguel tried to sound offended, but the proximity of his face to mine and how conflicted his eyes were told two different stories. "You're not listening to me."

My eyes drifted to my back pocket. Meechie was probably texting me. The coast was clear now, most of the parking lot empty.

I took a chance to get closer, and Miguel seized it as always, pulling me in.

He was getting on my nerves with his lack of respect for the concept of personal space, but it wasn't like I could stay mad. I was just as addicted to his tender touch as he seemed to be. I was just ten times more aware of who was and wasn't paying attention.

"I know what I want. I want us to…" My voice failed me.

"To what?" He tried to get me to press on, squeezing my hand slightly.

Date died on my lips before I could even form the word. What if he said he wasn't interested? Or gave me that exasperated look again, that I was over-complicating everything.

He'd just make more accusations, get more distant, look at me like I was being annoying.

And I didn't want that. I wanted him to look at me like I meant everything to him, to hold me close and kiss me so hard it felt like he was desperate and I was the only one who could make him feel good.

I tried to search Miguel's eyes for an answer, for confirmation that he might feel the same way, but I only found more questions reflected back at me.

What was the opposite of heavy? Light, right? So I'd keep things light.

"I want us to... be together. To have fun. *Relax*. Get closer. Eat lunch together. Explore the town some more. Have more amazing sex but not fuck up our client's house in the process. Is that all doable, you think? I'm sorry, okay? I just need to take things *slow*." And I put extra emphasis on slow. "And then we can figure out the hard parts later."

I continued with a shaky breath, "You wear your heart on your sleeve. I don't think you notice how... obvious we seem to everybody."

"Who cares what other people think if this is what we want? We're both adults."

He made a very good point. But I did care what other people thought of us, about me. And what if someday we stopped this, what then? I was getting ahead of myself, I knew that. But just because all that didn't matter to him, it didn't change the fact that it did to me.

"I get it, but I don't really know anyone out here. I don't... want to make things harder for him more than me."

I scanned the parking lot again. Empty. Good.

Miguel took a second to process what I was saying, and then his whole demeanor changed, his gaze less conflicted, more gentle.

"People can be more accepting than you think," he said with a sigh. "Gaynor Beach isn't as close minded as you probably think. It'll be okay."

I just nodded in return.

"I want us to get closer. I want you, Miguel. But let's just take things slow."

Miguel didn't seem satisfied with that, but he relented nonetheless. But as he went to leave, to pull away, he hesitated, so I closed the distance between our lips, savoring his taste, and his scent before he pulled away with a grin, still hugging.

But as we parted fully, the loss of his warmth left me shivering in the autumn cold. My heart was racing, faster than my thoughts. And despite every attempt to avoid the obvious, I knew I was falling head over heels for Miguel.

But I couldn't press my luck. I couldn't destroy something else that felt so good in my life. I would take things slow, and hopefully, one day, he'd see that we could be so much more. That a relationship, even settling down, didn't have to be *heavy*.

I pulled him in close. "Think I should see if Meechie wants to hang out with his friends tonight?"

He tilted his head to the side slightly, hair in his eyes, and I could feel my heart in my throat. Was I coming on too hard after what was most definitely our first fight, no matter how he spun it?

"You don't have to stay the night! Just come over for a little while."

Spontaneous, unlike me. Opening up way too much, too, which was scary.

I felt a sense of relief wash over me when he finally nodded enthusiastically.

"Lead the way."

CHAPTER 18

MIGUEL

DEMETRIUS' HOUSE WAS JUST LIKE THE MAN HIMSELF: ORDERLY and clean with a hint of warmth underlying. Nothing was out of place, but the couch was comfortable, with thick cushions, and the throw and pillows looked well worn. There was a light scent of spice in the air, like cinnamon candles or pumpkin lattes.

The Demetrius I knew behind closed doors was warm and open and sexual behind an orderly exterior, and I loved that his place was the same way.

"Do you want a drink?" he asked.

I nodded, if only so I could snoop on his kitchen too.

It looked so much more lived in than my place. His house was probably older than mine was, but it wasn't that. This was where Meech had left his school project on the table. There were a couple dishes in the sink, magnets and pictures on the fridge, including one of him, Meech, and his mother. I remembered her from the picture Demetrius showed me at the pier with her co-worker.

They made a beautiful family, and Meech looked a bit younger with the type of huge smile that he rarely gave now.

"It must be hard on him," I said.

Demetrius glanced over from pouring a glass of wine and saw what I was looking at.

"It is. They FaceTime, but it's not the same. He's always sad after they hang up their calls."

"What about you?" I asked.

He handed over a glass and I took it, swishing it while I watched him.

He smiled.

"To be honest, I don't really want to talk about my ex-wife anymore. Not with you."

I was stung for a moment until I saw the look in his eyes.

"Oh, I see. You would rather I help you forget her?" I teased.

A slow, sensuous smile lifted his lips, and I nearly dropped my glass, I forgot about it so fast.

I set it down and reached out, catching him by the front of his shirt, and tugged him in. My arms went around him, pulling his warm body tight against mine with a soft moan.

"How do you always feel so good?" I grumbled. "So sexy even with all your clothes on."

I kissed him and he melted into my embrace, his lips parting and tongue sliding against mine, quickly turning it filthy.

"Couch," I mumbled into his mouth, pushing him in that direction, but he fought against me, eventually pulling away and gripping me by the hand.

"Bed," he corrected, pulling me towards the stairs with a reproachful look.

I chuckled and let him lead the way.

The windows were open in his room, letting in the cool autumn air. Of course, his bed was made, the thick duvet tucked in with the precision I'd only ever seen in upscale hotels.

As soon as the door was closed, he gripped me by the hips, pulling our bodies together and smiling at me.

"What's on the menu for the day?" he asked playfully.

"Hm..." I wondered, hands slipping down, squeezing his ass. "For starters, we have making out naked."

"Sounds good," he laughed and reached for his shirt, pulling it eagerly off over his head. How he found time to keep so fit in between work and being a full-time single father, I had no idea, but I wasn't complaining.

I traced my fingers over his chest, his abs, and then dipped down, sucking a nipple between my lips.

He moaned, arching towards me. I reached for the other, rubbing it before switching my mouth to that side, sucking on the tight nub while he shuddered, gripping my shoulders.

"Oh. I didn't know that was so—"

His phone suddenly rang, loud and unwelcome in the room.

Knowing him well enough to read the look in his eyes, I was ready when he reached into his pocket, pushing him back so that he fell onto the bed with a yelp.

"Hey, it might be the plumber."

"Fuck the plumber," I said, crawling over him while he struggled to pull his phone out. I tugged my shirt off just as he pulled it free from his pocket. He lifted it to his face, but I quickly tugged it out of his hand and tossed it to the side, pulling his face towards me when he reached for it.

The second our eyes met, he shook his head.

"You're so pushy."

"We were in the middle of something," I reminded him, brushing my lips against his, just enough to tease. "The menu, remember?"

He gave a breathy chuckle.

"I believe you were about to tell me the main course?"

"Mmhm," I agreed, biting his bottom lip and running my tongue along it. He moaned, hands sliding up my back and tangling into my hair.

"It's me," I finally whispered. "If you want."

He followed my lips as I pulled away, eager for more, but then stopped, head flopping back onto the mattress to look up at me.

"You mean... ?"

I laughed. It was cute that he wouldn't say it, just in case he was wrong.

"Yes," I said, kissing him again. "You haven't tried it yet. Do you want to fuck me?"

"Yes," he said immediately and then pulled me down for another deep kiss. "Hell yes."

His hands slid down, gripping my ass, holding me in place and then he ground up into me.

I gasped. He moaned. And then another sound reached our ears.

A small voice called Demetrius' name.

For a second, we stared at each other in confusion, and then, with a look of disbelief, Demetrius reached for his phone.

It was lying face up by our hips and I could see that it was on a call as he lifted it up and read the name: *Denise*.

Her voice on the other end was louder now and clear as day.

"Tri? Is that seriously you? What the hell? Who are you with? Answer me!"

He hung up.

His hands were shaking so hard that I thought he might drop the phone. And he was growing softer by the second, eyes wide with panic, breaths shallow.

Slowly, he lowered the phone. I could think of nothing else to do but hug him, so I did, dropping my head next to his and kissing his cheek.

"Was that her?" I asked. "Your ex, I mean."

He nodded mutely. I could feel his heart pounding against my chest.

"Demetrius," I whispered. "I'm so sorry."

"Get off me," he choked.

Grimacing, I rolled away.

He was up instantly, pacing and wringing his hands, nearly hyperventilating. Something like gloom and foreboding sank down, engulfing me while I watched, unsure what to do.

"She's your ex," I said, and the fact that I suddenly felt like he needed to be reminded hurt.

He didn't seem to hear me and then, suddenly, he swung around to face me, expression twisted in anger.

"I told you I wanted to take that call."

"If it was the plumber," I said, rising, "but it wasn't."

"No. It was Denise. I should have answered it. And *not* accidentally. She doesn't like when I ignore her."

"Demetrius, you're not together anymore. You don't owe her anything."

"I do. You don't understand," he argued. "You should have waited. I told you I wanted to answer it."

I blinked.

"I'm hoping you weren't planning on talking to your ex while we were fucking."

He cringed, like the idea of it said out loud was too much. And he never would say it, would he? He liked to pretend it wasn't happening, this thing between us. Maybe because it was too hard, or maybe it was because he didn't like that it *was* happening.

I swallowed, straightening to my full height. Yes, he was taller, but not by much. And although sometimes it didn't seem like it, I was older, wiser even. I'd been here before, I'd been the guy who wasn't wanted, who wasn't good enough, and I wouldn't be him again.

But... for the sake of the sheer amount that I adored this guy, I tried one more time.

"You were with her—*Denise*—for a long time. Is she homophobic?"

He stared at me for a long time. Finally, he shook his head minutely.

I reached out and gripped him by both shoulders.

"It's okay then," I said. "She'll understand, right? You're not together anymore and you're with a guy, but she's *not* homophobic. Maybe she'll be surprised, but that's it. Right?"

I was hoping for a shaky head nod at the very least.

Instead, Demetrius shook my hands off and walked to the bed. He sat gingerly on the edge, not looking at me.

"Please leave."

His words, the finality in his voice, instantly crushed me.

I didn't move.

For probably a full minute, I thought of staying, of fighting, of forcing him to love me.

"Are you sure?" I asked, hoping he would understand, that I would get through to him. "If you want me to go for your ex that you don't even see anymore…"

I swallowed.

"What?" he asked sharply, suddenly looking up and meeting my gaze. "Are you going to give me an ultimatum or something?"

I didn't know what to say.

"That's rich coming from you," he went on. "You don't care about anything but yourself, do you?"

That was the final blow.

I managed to keep it together long enough to scoop my shirt off the floor before I left. The front door wasn't so lucky.

It slammed hard enough that the windows rattled on my way out. Instantly, I felt guilty. I didn't want to cause a scene in Meech's house or destroy it; I just wanted this feeling gone.

No amount of aggression would manage that.

As a younger man, I would have thrown things, kicked rocks down the street, and punched walls.

I remembered what that was like: instant pain relief, a

brief distraction, followed by gloom. Anger gone, and sadness left unavoidable in its place.

Nothing would free me from the fact that Demetrius didn't want me.

I'd known all along that the breakup from his wife had been hard. For some reason, the idea that Demetrius could still be in love with her hadn't been something I could face.

Now, seeing how much he cared about her knowing, and how much more important she was than me made me feel sick.

I knew he had known her for years. I knew our relationship was still new and delicate. That didn't stop it from hurting.

CHAPTER 19

DEMETRIUS

I was a mess for far too long after Miguel left, my heart racing, mind a maze of anxiety leading to dead end after dead end as I tried to figure out what to do next.

What did it matter if Denise was homophobic or not? She heard me *fucking* someone over the phone, as Miguel had so cruelly pointed out.

I'd be disgusted if she did something like that to me. Wouldn't anybody? And what if she didn't just get over it? What then?

My shaky hands roamed the bed, finally registering the ringing in my ears as not my blood pressure spiking but the fact that my phone was ringing off the hook.

It could be her, or Miguel, or even Meechie asking when he could come home. I had to answer it, but as I held it face down in my hands, I couldn't bring myself to flip my phone over and look at the screen.

Everything was still too fresh to just hope it all blew over and worked out for the best. I already felt like I was walking on eggshells, and now I went and made such a stupid mistake. And Miguel, as always, seemed to think it was no big deal. Like he'd be laughing if the situation was

144

reversed and he was fresh off a divorce balancing custody of his son.

Maybe he would. I felt like I really didn't know him then. I figured he'd try to comfort me, but I honestly just wanted to be alone to collect my thoughts. Not be given an ultimatum. As if I wouldn't have to face Denise ever again. She wasn't some childhood friend; she was my son's mother.

And his mother was moving out to San Diego to be closer to her son, which meant we'd be interacting a lot more than just a phone call to arrange a plane ride every other summer or some shit. Our shared custody arrangement meant sharing a significant portion of our lives, forever.

But I couldn't exactly throw that in Miguel's face, could I? One, because he'd left, like I'd asked him to so there was that. Two, because he'd just look at me with the same accusation in his eyes. Like I was making a huge stank over my ex in front of my boyfriend, and not my FWB.

Shit!

"We're not even dating…" I sighed, the weight of that fact causing my hands to shake even more.

Why would Miguel be thinking long term anyway? About navigating co-parenting and making sure our relationship stayed amicable?

We weren't dating. And, as I finally mustered up the courage to turn my phone around, it was becoming painfully clear to me we might never get to chance to progress to more than just fuck buddies.

I didn't know who's name I hoped would flash across the screen, but it was in fact Denise who finally stopped blowing up my phone, leaving a short voicemail.

My thumb hovered over the play button, and finally, with a deep breath, I hit play.

The message was curt, her voice strained: "You know what, don't answer! I really don't know why the fu… Ugh, whatever. Listen, I don't want to talk about this over the phone. But call me back because you know I'm flying in soon and I need to know if I need to rent a car, if you're dropping off Meechie. Just... Actually, no. Leave me a message, *Demetrius*. Bye."

Click. I deleted the evidence as soon as she was finished. She practically spat my name. A ragged sigh left my throat, and I slowly fell back on the bed, my phone resting on my chest. It was all so fucking embarrassing.

How was I going to explain this? *Oops, I accidentally answered you in bed* wasn't going to fly. I should just apologize, I was going to apologize, when we eventually met face to face.

"Ha," a cruel laugh, more like a huff of hot air left me, "and just hope it works out."

My bed felt too large, and I felt too naked and exposed, dick limp and heart thudding out of control. I got up and pulled on some pajamas, dark gray sweats passable as a workout outfit if I had to still go out tonight to pick up Meechie. Though I hoped he could just spend the night at Nate's.

Pacing, thinking, sighing. I was doing everything but leaving that message to coordinate with Denise. Avoidance, something I never used to do and now I couldn't stop doing it.

I kept glancing at my phone that I'd left face up on the bed. I wanted to call her, to make things right. But even more so, I wanted to call *him*.

To apologize, because this time around I really did feel like I needed to. He had just tried to comfort me, in his "it's-never-as-serious-as-you-think" Miguel type of way. But still, he'd offered comfort. Maybe I should've swallowed my fear and just played along with him.

But as I paused, hand hovering over the screen, waffling between running after him and calling, I finally accepted that this *thing* between us... Maybe it just couldn't work.

I was known to put the cart before the wheel, but this time I went out and brought the whole damn horse too. I was already planning so far ahead, worried about the perfect moment to confess I wanted something more. But when was I given any indication that that was what Miguel wanted?

He wanted affection, publicly. Sex, often. And fun, family-centric time on occasion. All great things. But he never talked about the hard stuff with me. About the nitty-gritty of what happened if we took things a step further.

He wanted a good time, and I thought I did too, until this. No, I wanted something deeper. I wanted more than a hug and pat on the shoulder that things would be okay. Like we could go back to this new normal of being more than friends, but nothing more, after this.

Love took commitment, compromising, and probably another word that started with *c* I couldn't think of at the moment. And then there was parenting. God, my stomach sank just thinking about introducing him to Denise. Not because Miguel was a man, though a part of me was worried about that too. It was a big change after all.

But the real fear was thinking how they wouldn't get along, and then what? A dragged-out fight in court over custody? I didn't want that. Not one fucking bit when every-thing was going so well with her relocating and moving on, and me finding someone new, too, who really bonded with Meechie.

Maybe I was catastrophizing. Another word I learned from my very expensive, and currently useless, therapy sessions. But I'd been with Denise long enough to know her by now. Some things could be treated like water under the bridge, but to her this would be seen as the ultimate disre-spect. Something she didn't take kindly to even now, older and calmer. She used to smack bitches for less, in her words, when she was younger and wilder back in school.

How would she react when she stepped off that plane, and Meechie was out of sight in the backseat of the car?

I sat down on the edge of my bed, head in my hands, back to square one. The more I thought about it, the more upset I became. I wiped at my cheek.

I was crying? Yes, as much as I didn't want to acknowledge it, I was hurt. Wounded, even.

It was too soon to be putting my heart and my new life on the line for a good time. There was already so much I needed to take care of, responsibilities that wouldn't just disappear. It was unfair for me to expect more from Miguel when that was never the arrangement in the first place. And worst of all, I'd already dragged my son into it all.

It's time I end whatever I got going on with Miguel. I knew I'd regret letting go and giving in. I didn't know ending would feel so painful. It's all my fault, again...

CHAPTER 20

MIGUEL

THE CLOSER MONDAY CAME, THE MORE MY ANXIETY ROSE.

I caved on Sunday evening and dialed Demetrius' number with my heart in my throat. He declined the call on the first ring. A text followed that I couldn't help sending.

Will we be okay working together?

No response.

A fitful night of sleep didn't help matters.

I woke up panda-eyed and stressed, my heart in my throat as though something truly terrible had happened.

It was the family aspect, I realized, and that only made it burn worse as I drove to work. Demetrius had felt like he just fit straight into my life and my heart. With him and Meech, I had jumped in head first. I felt like they were my family.

It was ridiculous. It hadn't even been a month yet. Close, but not quite and Demetrius and I had only been intimate for a couple of weeks now.

Remembering the sneaked touches on site brought a sad smile to my lips.

Why was I so invested?

Maybe I could convince him—*no.* I wouldn't do that. If he didn't want me, I wouldn't chase.

But God, what I wouldn't give to walk on site and have Demetrius walk up to me, embrace me in the open and tell the world that he'd made a stupid mistake out of fear.

I had to push the fantasy away as I parked across the street from the house. For a moment, I just sat and looked up at it.

The new windows, front steps, and paint job had already upgraded the property immensely. It was looking a hundred times better than it had when we'd first arrived months ago to start the project. Inside, it still looked like a construction site, but it was moving fast. Another month, maybe two, and we would be done. Winchelsea House and all the memories I'd made inside of it would be gone.

I was early, as usual, but I couldn't face going in yet and pretending everything was fine.

Instead, I dialed Dan's number, knowing he would be up.

"Miguel!" he answered, a smile in his voice, and instantly, I felt a little bit better. "How's it going? It took you too long to give me a ring."

I chuckled.

"I got distracted," I said honestly. I'd been so preoccupied by Demetrius. "How are you? How is your family? Are the kids settling into their new school?"

"They absolutely hate it," he admitted, launching into detail about the moving drama, how half their furniture took an extra two days to arrive and the whole family had had to sleep in one bed—and Perry was a kicker.

I was laughing when he enthusiastically told me about Perry kicking him in the face while they were sleeping on the second night and how he'd had to show up for his first day on his new job with a shiner.

That, of course, led to asking about work.

"It's fine here," he said. "Nice guys and the current project is a lot more simple than Winchelsea House, but, you know, it's not the same without you three. I miss your stupid faces."

I smiled sadly, hearing the truth under the gentle jab.

"We miss you too," I sighed. "*I* miss you guys. I feel like my family left me."

Dan sighed.

"It sucks, doesn't it? But hey, you can still come visit, and we'll come to you too."

"Yeah," I agreed, knowing it wasn't the same.

"I've never heard you sounding so down," he suddenly said. "Is everything else okay? Work? The new PM? What's he like?"

Right on cue, Demetrius arrived, not seeing me as he climbed the steps to enter the house. I bit my lip, watching him.

"He's like you said, a stickler for things being done right but… I like him."

"Yeah?" Dan asked, not sounding convinced.

"Probably too much," I admitted.

"Really?" Dan asked, interest piqued. "He must be pretty great to catch your eye, Miguel. You're a serious catch."

I knew he meant it, but it still made me laugh.

"Yes, well, he doesn't seem to think so at the moment."

"Then he's not worth your time."

Dan was good for offering all the platitudes a good friend would. I wanted to tell him the whole story if only so he could comfort me, but time was ticking and I was about to be late.

"I have to head in," I sighed.

"Me too," he admitted. "I've been sitting outside my work for the last five minutes."

I laughed.

"Same."

"Before I hang up," he said, voice suddenly serious, "don't get too hung up on someone who doesn't give you everything, Miguel. Seriously, you're a great guy and you deserve someone who sees that."

I took a shaky breath and forced an agreement out of my lips before saying goodbye.

Maybe Demetrius didn't see it in me, that I would be a good fit, but I saw it in him. How was I supposed to just forget that?

Collecting myself, I got up, unpacked my gear, and went inside.

Demetrius was like the man from his first week again, cold and stoic with a quick hello as he went straight to his office. He barely even glanced in my direction.

I was in darkness for the rest of the day. Sometimes I would get angry, but mostly I was just sad, deep-diving into thoughts about my past for some reason, seeing things coming together as though on a string.

I'd never wanted commitment. I'd burned Maria early, the same way that Demetrius was doing to me now. When Rodrigo had cheated, I'd taken it as a sign to remain easy and open to all that life had to offer. To not expect anything.

For years I'd remained single out of stubbornness, I now realized. If I didn't get my hopes up, I wouldn't get hurt.

But I'd thought Demetrius was different.

How was I just learning this about myself now? I was almost forty and just figuring myself out. Worst of all, it felt like I'd wasted years not understanding myself. Not understanding how much I wanted someone in my bed each night to hold and wake up with for breakfast and adventures. To travel with and love day in and out. The addition of a child too... that was the dream. A big happy family. The kind I'd never had.

I worked through lunch, unwilling to stop and pretend to be happy while Chris and Mike chatted away.

I managed to make it to the end of the day with barely a word to anyone. Relieved and exhausted, I packed my tools into my truck.

That was when the guys ambushed me.

I was still lost in thought, eager to get home, and didn't notice either of them until they were blocking the way to the driver's door.

I froze.

"What the hell is going on with you two?" Mike asked.

I knew exactly who else he was talking about. My lips parted to say something but nothing came out.

"Is everything okay?" Chris asked.

I swallowed and somehow managed a nod.

"Sure. I don't know what you're talking about."

They glanced at each other. Mike rolled his eyes and Chris shook his head, and suddenly, I wondered if we were as discrete as we'd thought we were.

"Okay, if you wanna keep pretending you're not hooking up with Demetrius, that's fine. Just tell us why you're both so quiet today."

I grimaced.

I could only imagine how Demetrius would feel if he heard them.

"Sh," I hushed, gaze flying to the house. Demetrius hadn't left yet and there was no sign of him.

Then I looked at their expectant faces and sighed.

"Look, he's not out. Neither of you know any of this."

"You might have wanted to think of that before making out against the framing in the basement. Seriously, there wasn't even any drywall to hide you."

I felt my cheeks heat and shook my head.

"You. Saw. *Nothing*."

"Seriously," Chris chimed in. "Hooking up at work. That's way worse than drinking."

"What did I just say?" I demanded.

He held his hands up innocently.

"I saw nothing."

Just then the door opened and Demetrius stood on the top step.

He looked like a freaking angel standing up there in his clean-cut clothes, the sun on his shoulders and hair.

"Hey, Miguel, while you're still here, do you have a minute?"

I shoved past the guys while they snickered. My chest and stomach were tight with nerves. Something about the look on Demetrius' face set me on edge.

He didn't look happy. Resigned maybe.

The second the front door was closed behind us, I turned to him.

"Is everything okay?" I asked, then, remembering what the guys had so easily spied us doing, added, "Let's go to your office."

He shook his head, not watching me.

"No. This won't take long."

"What is it?" I asked. I reached for him, unable to help myself, but he shifted away before I could.

My hand dropped.

"We have to end this," he said, just like that. No lead in, no softening what I already knew was happening.

I swallowed.

"Demetrius—"

"I wanted to put it out there, make it official, that's all."

"That's all?" I repeated.

He nodded.

My eyes suddenly stung, but I blinked it back, fighting to remain calm.

I had to bite the insides of my cheeks and take a deep breath to summon the ability to react calmly, but I could barely keep it together even then.

Finally, I shrugged, backing towards the door, eager to get the hell out of here before he had to deal with me in tears.

"Whatever makes you happy," I said.

I didn't slam the door behind me this time.

The guys were gone, thankfully. Maybe they thought I

would have been in there longer. Maybe they thought me and Demetrius were going to have sex on the new marble countertops before moving to his office for more.

I felt a little sick when I got in the driver's side door.

Making a breakup official was the decent thing to do. That was what everyone said. but it hurt like hell and I wished he'd just let me wallow without saying it.

I started the engine, taking off even though my sight was blurry with stinging tears.

Demetrius would come outside any second now, and I didn't want to be here blubbering like an idiot when he did.

CHAPTER 21

DEMETRIUS

WORK WAS HELL FOR THE REST OF THE WEEK, ALL THE WAY UP TO Friday evening. There was no other way to put it. I kept my head down, stayed on the phone, doing anything but dealing with what I had caused.

It didn't make me happy to end things, far from it; I was fucking depressed.

But just as easy breezy as he strode into my life, Miguel had walked out, shrugging his shoulders, and that was that.

He was angry, I could tell. Anyone could see that, even the guys who I had to force myself to pretend didn't know something was up.

Yes, angry, but not overly emotional past that. We kept our distance. Got the job done. And went home without a word. We finally factory reset our relationship, only we ended up blowing up the TV in the process.

How a month-long fling hurt almost as much as a divorce was a mystery to me. Maybe because I'd placed so much hope on this working out after everything else came crashing down.

At least I ended things on my terms, I told myself as I packed up to leave. It was a cold comfort, but it made me feel less pathetic to keep holding out hope for some Hollywood production where he stepped up and said all the things I wanted to hear. Or I grew the balls to say it instead.

I shook my head. No point dwelling on things that weren't going to change.

It would take time, but I'd come to terms with it all soon enough. Things had moved too fast, and I got too caught up in my emotions to see reality.

Now I was back in control, fully, of my life. For better and for worse.

Leaving as soon as I could, I was happy to switch back to dad mode for a change. Meechie had been so busy between after school activities and soccer practice that he hadn't had much time to relax with me.

"I'm home," I said, my smile faltering when I saw Denise's face greeting me at the door.

I halted by the door in shock, only recovering when I noticed Meechie bouncing off the walls.

He held up his tablet with her face on it, grinning ear to ear. "Mom said she'll be here in time for my away game! And Halloween!"

I quickly forced a huge smile, nodding, and thankfully Denise did the same. Though hers looked more sincere. She'd always been better at masking her emotions.

On top of avoiding Miguel, I'd been avoiding Denise's calls for a week as well. She'd already sent over her flight information, her hotel, and all the details that I needed. It was cowardly, I knew, but I just didn't have it in me to call her back and potentially face a meltdown.

But now we were face to virtual face, and there was no avoiding her.

"Dad! Mom's coming this weekend." He repeated himself, like I didn't hear him the first time.

Though I had zoned out, so it might have seemed like it. I

closed the door behind me gingerly, fidgeting with the doorknob.

"That's… wonderful! I can't wait."

I was lying through my fucking teeth.

But Meechie didn't seem to notice, flipping the tablet around as he rambled about soccer practice, and his new friend Quinten and how cool his older brother Kordell and dad Nate were, and how much he missed Denise, Grandpa, and Grandma. Asking if they were coming to Gaynor for Christmas, or if we were going back to Bethesda. If my parents would move closer to Gaynor too, so we weren't so far away from each other.

A ragged sigh tore through me that I muffled with a cough, shuffling towards the kitchen while Meechie roamed around the hall.

I made myself busy in the kitchen, making dinner, trying not to listen but forced to anyway. Meechie decided to sit in the living room, making me in earshot of their call, my back probably visible to her.

Denise responded in an upbeat tone, but a little withdrawn. Probably just as aware of the fact I could hear them chatting away as she could.

Locking my gaze on the sizzling chicken on the stove top, preparing chicken alfredo, I tried to ignore them just for a little while. Until Meechie unknowingly set a disaster in motion.

"And… Oh, oh! When you come, you can meet Miguel."

My heart skipped, nearly knocking over my tongs as I went to stir the pasta.

"Who's Miguel?"

And there it was. The other shoe dropped. I could practically hear her teeth grinding over the line, though I knew Denise was probably still wearing a sweet smile.

Had she noticed how deep the other voice was on the

phone? She must've, because she wouldn't sound upset over me having a male friend otherwise.

"Dad's new friend! He's really nice. You'll like him. We go *everywhere* together. He drove us around when Dad crashed the car. Miguel took us to the fair and this haunted house thing. Dad, is Miguel coming to my away game?"

I swallowed hard, calling over my shoulder, "No, he can't make it."

His head poked over the couch, frowning. I quickly turned away; Denise's eyes narrowed on the tablet screen.

"Why not?"

"He just… can't." It was all I could manage.

"What about the picnic? The parade? Trick-or-treating?"

What happened to turning off the implosion of my relationship with Miguel and just being dad for a change?

Oh right, that would've only worked if he hadn't woven himself into the fabric of our new lives. If I hadn't encouraged it and longed for it.

Shit.

"He can't. We're, um, really busy with the house and he's pretty busy too with other things. How about you say goodbye to Mom for now. We'll see you Sunday, okay?"

I was practically begging Meechie to hang up, stuff his face, and forget about Miguel for just one second. Plus, it was getting late back on the East Coast, given the time difference. A perfect excuse.

But he pressed on. "I think he'll come. He always does! Just call him and see. Maybe we can trick-or-treat later in the day so he can make it. Or me and Mom can, and we have a picnic in the morning? Whatever. He just has to come to the parade with us at least!"

"O-Okay. We'll figure it out. Let's say goodnight. You know it's really late back home."

Finally, Meechie relented. We said our goodbyes, and then

he grabbed himself a plate for dinner and got to work inhaling his food.

I sat at the dinner table picking at my food, mind a mess. My eyes flicked to the top of the fridge, where Meechie demanded I display the scarecrow pumpkin doll from the Autumn Fair.

A beautiful day, and memory, that just happened to also be with Miguel. There were so many of them now, too many fond memories of us, together, and this town. Pieces of him scattered throughout our lives now. But then one mistake ruined it all.

————

THE WEEKEND DRAGGED ON, ALMOST AS PAINFUL AS MY WEEK AT work. I was fleeing one battle for another, worried that I was going to get into a fight with Denise.

All I could do was pray she had enough sense to save it for when we were alone and not in front of our son.

The trip from Gaynor Beach was largely uneventful. The vibrant evening sky I'd grown used to faded to a brilliant shade of blue once we made it to San Diego.

Then, we arrived at San Diego International Airport about thirty minutes earlier than Denise's flight. I listened mutely as Meechie talked up a storm in the backseat, asking about every five minutes where Mom's plane was.

Then, finally, the moment of reckoning was here.

Denise stepped through the doors, just as I remembered: dark-skinned with thick, kinky black locs, sharp brown eyes, and curves for days. She was dressed more stylishly, though, a form-fitting red dress that looked vaguely like an airplane attendant uniform. Very different compared to her usual airport attire of sweatpants and a graphic tee. She was balancing a carry-on and two rolling suitcases with a huge smile.

Meechie and I got out at the same time, and I had to snatch him back from running into oncoming traffic. We waited for her to come to us, and then I let him go.

"Mommy!" Meechie buried his face in her waist, buzzing with excitement.

It caught me by surprise. He'd woken up one day and we suddenly went from Mommy and Daddy to Mom and Dad. I suspected he got teased at school. Despite not showing it, Meechie was a sensitive kid, overly aware of what others thought of him. A lot like his dad.

So to see him shouting "Mommy" made me smile and feel sad. They'd been separated for far too long. A month didn't seem like a long time, until now.

"I missed you, baby. I got you an outfit for trick-or-treating," she said, dropping her suitcases as she scooped him up in a tight hug.

My fingers flexed by my side. Any other time, I'd join them, sandwiching them both in an even tighter hug. But I kept second-guessing myself until their moment was over, and I was helping her pack bags into the trunk and getting Meechie strapped back in for the ride to her hotel.

Denise paused by the passenger side door, tugging it open. I didn't know if I should say something, anything really, other than hello.

She closed the door suddenly, walking to me with slow, deliberate steps.

"Um, let me explain!" My voice strained, trying to stay quiet.

But instead of going off on me, her shoulders sank, and Denise sighed so hard she folded a little.

"You know, I sat on that plane the whole time, not sure what to do or what to say once I landed. But seeing Meechie, I guess that's all that really matters. I was just so... I know you'd never do that to me. Over one picture. And we... I don't know but just know it happened after us. But then... A man... I couldn't believe it! Ugh!"

Oh, oh, oh.

Things were happening too fast. There was so much I wanted to explain, but I was tongue tied.

Yes, I could tell something was going on with her and her co-worker.

No, I didn't think she cheated. She met her co-worker after we separated, after we divorced. Maybe they got together too fast, but who was I to talk, seeing as I had been with Miguel?

I would never do something wild and outlandish like record myself having sex to get back to her. This wasn't reality TV.

Yes... My new partner was a man. Maybe, seeing as we weren't together anymore.

Fuck.

But I couldn't force any of that out of my mind past my throat, cotton mouthed. My eyes darted to Meechie, who looked at us impatiently from the back window.

Slapping both of her cheeks, Denise rolled her eyes skyward like she was sending up a silent prayer.

"...We can talk, when you're ready. When we're both ready. Okay? For now, let's just... let's just have some quality family time, and give me some time to get my shit together, too. For him."

I nodded, dumbfounded but thankful she didn't cause a scene. That she didn't push the topic any further, though there was so much left to be said. A bit of grace could go a long way.

"Thank you... I'll explain everything. When the time is right."

She nodded slowly, before getting inside my car. I released a shuddering breath, truly thankful. I was ready to get inside myself until my phone started buzzing.

I checked and was shocked to see Chris of all people was

calling me. I'd saved everyone's numbers, but it wasn't like Mike or Chris to call me after hours.

Maybe something had gone wrong in the house and they forgot to tell me?

"Hello?" I answered, holding up a finger to Denise, who cocked her head at me from the window.

"Hey," he said right away. "So... are you free? Later tonight, I mean."

"Maybe?" I said, knowing I would be but not sure what he was getting at.

"Well, if you are, Mike and I are kicking back at The Cantina for Oktoberfest. You should join us."

Was Miguel going would've been my next question, but he didn't mention him at all. Which was strange. I figured he was. They were his friends, after all.

An invitation sans Miguel seemed odd. But maybe Miguel was truly busy.

"Whaddya say?"

I glanced back at the car and found Denise happily chatting with Meechie, who was out of his seatbelt and hanging on the back of her seat. They'd be busy all night, catching up. And I wouldn't have to pick him up for school until later.

"...Okay, I'll be there around eight," I said, and after some enthusiastic grunts on Chris' end, we hung up.

It felt good to not be completely shut out. So why did I have such a bad feeling swirling around in my gut?

CHAPTER 22

MIGUEL

ALL WEEK I'D TRIED TO GET OUT OF THE OKTOBERFEST NIGHT OUT the boys wanted to do, but as I stepped into our usual haunt, The Gaynor Cantina, seeing the place decked out in autumnal decor, the sampler keg stations, and upbeat atmosphere, my mood lifted some.

Mike was already there, chatting up a storm with the bartender Evan.

Grinning, I approached.

Evan looked at me, shaking his head over his bowtie.

"We have to wear the uniforms," he informed me.

I leaned over the bar to see how far his lederhosen went and chuckled at the sight of his exposed knee-high socks.

"Adorable," I said.

He laughed and shrugged.

"I can pull it off anyway."

He poured me my beer and Mike watched me from the corner of his eye, his dark mustache lifting in a smirk.

I took the pint when Evan slid it over but waited for him to attend other patrons before raising a brow at Mike.

"What?" I demanded.

Mike shrugged.

"Good to see you laughing and smiling, that's all," he said.

I nodded, said smile dimming.

"Ah," he sighed. "Come on, forget about Demetrius. Let's drink."

We *clinked* our glasses together and somehow, I managed to fall into a conversation with him.

Chris arrived when I was on my fourth pint, laughing at a story Mike was telling me about the fishing trip I'd bailed on.

He announced himself by dropping an arm around my shoulders and giving me a friendly squeeze.

"Aw, he's smiling again! That's the Miguel I know."

I shoved him away playfully. It was a bit annoying that they kept bringing it up, but at the same time, I loved that they cared.

"What are you drinking?" Chris asked, waving Evan over.

"The usual."

Just then, another voice spoke behind me.

"Hey guys."

I froze, unable to look as shock filled me.

The boys said their hellos. Chris pulled out the stool next to him and then Demetrius took it and I was forced to see him.

He looked good, as usual. It looked like he'd had a haircut, his face was clean, his long-sleeved shirt in emerald green complemented his skin and those jeans complemented his ass, and I had to look away.

I downed the rest of my drink and waved for another.

Evan slipped me one, giving me a questioning look. Then his gaze shot to Demetrius sitting awkwardly next to Chris. He bit his lip, holding in a smile. Evan was so nosy. The perfect bartender.

Next to me, the small talk started, and I was seriously regretting getting this drink now because it meant I had to stay.

In my mind on repeat, I couldn't stop thinking about the last time I had been here. The first time I'd kissed Demetrius... the taste, the feel of his chest, rising and falling against mine, the look in his eyes in that bathroom stall.

He'd been the sexiest person alive that night, and I'd felt more alive than I ever had, just with him in my arms.

And now he was a seat over from me, talking to Chris as though it had never happened.

I couldn't talk. No, scratch that, I *wouldn't*.

Demetrius didn't give me the time of day anymore, so why should I give him mine?

At work, he barely spoke to me beyond what he needed me to do. In fact, he often deferred to Chris or Mike now unless it was something important. Aside from that, it was one-word answers and avoided looks.

If he didn't want to see me or talk to me, why the hell would he come out with me and my friends?

I sat tapping my foot, aware that an air of tension was being generated around me. Mike and Chris exchanged a look over me, and Demetrius twiddled his thumbs.

After a prolonged silence, Demetrius finally turned to me and Mike.

"Why are you here?" I asked, interrupting whatever he was about to say.

The words just slipped out of my mouth.

Mike sucked in a breath, muttering *ouch*, and Demetrius' face fell.

"Chris invited me."

I swiveled, giving Chris an accusatory look.

He shrugged innocently.

And here I'd thought the guys had been trying to force me out to help lift my spirits and get my mind off the breakup, but no. They were clueless and insensitive, and I didn't have to stay. So, I pushed up, surprised when I swayed just a little.

Forcing myself to remain steady, I picked up my beer and walked away, towards the band.

There wasn't much room for them. The Gaynor Cantina wasn't huge, but somehow, people always found room to squeeze up close to the players and dance.

I leaned against the wall first, finishing my drink, mood sour, gaze occasionally flying back to the bar where the others were still sitting and chatting.

One day, I would get over it. I'd learn to stop hating Demetrius for not wanting what I wanted, for kicking me out of what had felt like our own blossoming family... but today was not that day.

I felt peeled open and raw.

It was *weird* how surprised he had looked.

Did he really think I didn't care? That it wouldn't bother me to see him and hang out with him after he'd cut me loose like that?

I swallowed the rest of my drink and then stood there, torn between marching home and lying in bed miserable, or staying here just to spite the guy with my angry presence. The latter won.

I ordered another drink, avoiding their seats and not looking at them, then went back to the dance floor. This time I swayed and moved to the beat, letting the loud music wash through me, feeling the vibrations from the speakers that I was standing too close to. I was bound to lose my hearing early over the constant use of power tools anyway, so why not?

Somehow I managed to dance without spilling the entirety of my drink.

I took the last gulp of it and then, as I continued to sway with the empty glass in my hand, someone touched my back with one hand and pulled it gently from my grip with the other.

I turned, heart sinking to see Demetrius setting my glass

down on the nearest table before he turned to look at me, biting his lip and dammit, *why* did I still want to kiss him so badly? It was killing me.

I forced myself to stop dancing, stepping away from him.

"What do you want?" I asked.

He had to lean closer to be heard over the music. His body heat was like a magnet. Unconsciously, I started moving closer, unable to help myself.

"I thought we should talk," he said. "I don't want things to be awkward."

I laughed bitterly and he looked down for a moment, lips pursed before speaking again.

"I'll go," he said. "Go hang out with your friends. I don't want to ruin everyone's night."

That was rich. Acting like he was so considerate. If he'd cared about my feelings at all, he wouldn't have come tonight, as though we could just be normal now. Like nothing had happened. I couldn't do that. Not yet. In fact, the way I felt was ridiculous, like Demetrius had been everything to me. Like I was mourning the loss.

I shook my head.

"No. You stay. I'm leaving anyway."

"Miguel."

"I need air," I said and pushed past him, straight out the door.

There was so much I wanted to say to him. I half wanted to stay and rant just to get it off my chest. I wanted to tell him off, tell him he was an asshole for how he'd been acting at work. That he was stupid for flushing our growing relationship down the drain. Beyond that though, I still wanted to tell him the other things too, the things I hadn't had the chance to say, like how much I liked spending time with him, how much I wanted to be a part of his family, how deeply I was falling in love.

I blinked, throat tight as I stumbled to the road, looking up and down for a cab.

The noise from the bar, the upbeat music, and the happy voices from the patio felt so distant. Normally finding the best in each moment was my biggest skill. Right now, though, all I could focus on was how hurt I felt.

Why had I decided to open my heart up to Demetrius after all these years of protecting it so fiercely?

CHAPTER 23

DEMETRIUS

THIS NIGHT COULDN'T BE GOING ANY WORSE. AFTER MIGUEL unceremoniously stumbled out of the bar—did he realize how drunk he was?—I found myself throwing fitful glances to the door and back at the guys, feeling betrayed that they led me into an ambush.

I felt anxious and deeply uneasy. And, more than anything, confused at how angry Miguel seemed to be.

I didn't expect us to be chummy; far from it, I figured we'd act the same tonight as we did during work once my eyes landed on him and I realized Chris hadn't been so forthcoming about why they were inviting me out. Cold, distant, with an undercurrent of animosity.

But not *this*. Like I broke his heart or something.

I had a small bit of hope that we'd have a chance to patch things over drinks. It would take time, but it would be alright eventually. Once I stopped running away, because at some point I had to.

We were grown. People hooked up and stopped all the time. Hadn't Miguel basically admitted to doing the same after his last boyfriend broke his heart?

Still, it was hard to see his handsome face twist up with

actual hatred, not anger, as he swayed on the dance floor, looking just as sexy as he'd ever been, and noticed me. I wasn't trying to make things worse. I figured Mike or Chris would intervene, but they kept chatting with the bartender, acting oblivious to *their* old friend getting wasted.

Was I just supposed to stand by and watch? Apparently so as I finally took a seat again, ready to drink. Lukewarm piss was still lukewarm piss, but it was better than sitting here with an empty stomach.

"A beer," I told the bartender, avoiding Mike and Chris's gaze.

I didn't really know what to say afterward. And my mind circled back to the obvious. Mike and Chris were Miguel's friends. This was his company. His life that I was now too wrapped up in. The gnawing feeling of emptiness ate away at me, the prospect of being alone again pressing.

Even the bartender seemed to notice the souring mood. Moments after I downed my first beer, I knew it would be my last. I needed to get out of here.

"I'm going to head out. Thanks," I finally managed, getting up and ready to head out.

But before I could get up and do what I did best back then, run away, Chris pulled me back down, as Mike turned to look at me fully.

"Look, I know it's not my place to say anything but whatever the hell went wrong with you two, just fix it, okay? I don't know how you and Miguel went from not being able to keep your hands off each other to this, but it's pretty dramatic, don't you think?"

I was gonna be sick. I knew they knew by now, but I didn't need them to say it.

He squinted at me, like he was really looking at me for the first time. "Miguel isn't an idiot," was what he finally settled on.

"I know that." What was the point of this conversation

other than to confirm we had definitely fooled around too much on the job?

"He wouldn't be fucking around on the job like that if you didn't mean something to him. And he isn't heartless. He wouldn't... He wouldn't be that fucked up over you if it didn't mean anything to him. Whatever you two had going on obviously meant something to him. So fix it and save us months of the silent treatment."

Oh.

I pulled my arm away. The room grew quiet as I tuned out the band, chatter, and clinking glasses. Gears started turning slowly in my head, circling back to a conclusion that made me breathless, and even more anxious.

Had I just... misunderstood him? Not picked up on some silent cue that this wasn't just a fling?

I couldn't have. No way.

But it seemed so obvious, if Chris and Mike would go out of their way to force us together in such a haphazard manner. To tell me that *we* meant more to Miguel than what I thought beforehand.

But Chris wasn't the guy I wanted to hear this from.

I wanted to hear it from Miguel.

"I'll see you guys." I left in a hurry, and this time neither of them tried to stop me.

It was getting surprisingly cold for a beach town as I hit the streets, eyes scanning the patio and partygoers. Miguel couldn't have gotten too far in his state.

I don't know what I was hoping for, what I was even planning to say. But I needed to find him. To see if Chris was right or if everything that happened between us was truly a lost cause.

"Miguel?" I asked, tight-lipped as he cast a glare over his shoulder.

He'd gotten to the end of the curb, leaning on a light post, trying to hail a cab.

"I can drive you home." My offer hung in the air and went unanswered.

A bad case of déjà vu. Somehow, our roles had reversed.

He murmured, too low for me to really understand. Something about a "finding a cab" I figured as he kept scanning the streets, then reaching for his phone.

I tried to touch him, my body reacting before my thoughts could catch up.

I wanted to hold him so badly, to hear him say that I meant more to him. To finally tell him all the things I kept bottled up, afraid of moving too fast, opening my heart to somebody so soon after it was broken. Scared that he wouldn't feel the same, and I'd have to deal with all these new, confusing thoughts and desires alone. That this time I'd shatter into pieces, too exposed, my heart too raw, unable to take a second blow so soon after the first.

But he shrugged me off, his voice hard as stone.

"Leave me alone, Demetrius. Just go."

I balled up my hand into a fist, which fell limply to my side. I had no idea how to react. The right words to say to get Miguel to listen eluded me. I wrapped my palm around my fist, biting my lower lip, closed my eyes, and turned away.

Running away, like a coward, again.

But just then, my phone buzzed in my back pocket. A message from Meechie. I opened it and couldn't help but smile. Denise and him were at some restaurant, and he had a stack of pancakes as tall as him: black, purple, orange, and slime green in the shape of jack-o-lanterns. He leaned into her side, his grin cut off by the way he had to angle the camera.

Way too much sugar this late at night. He'd be bouncing off the walls of the hotel.

Meechie: Mom loves it! We should bring Miguel next time!!

I blinked, the gears grinding in my mind.

Turning back around, I saw that Miguel had finally managed to flag down a cab. I had to act fast.

Rushing over, I grabbed his forearm and held, pushing through my anxiety and ignoring the look on his face.

"At least come to the parade. For Meechie's sake."

Not for me didn't have to be said. His frown deepened, gaze conflicted. And it made me feel like shit.

I knew I was guilt tripping him, being manipulative, and yet, I didn't care enough to stop. All I needed was one more chance, to see if what I was thinking was real. If we could still be more than friends, because I sure as hell couldn't stand the look in his eyes anymore. Like I was the enemy.

I wanted, no, needed a second chance.

"I just don't want you to disappear from his life."

He snorted, but this time he didn't snatch his arm out of my hand.

"But you sure want me gone from yours."

Ouch.

I shook my head no, mouth twisting up.

"No, that's not it."

"Then what is it?"

I bit the inside of my lip. If I kept chewing, I knew I'd draw blood.

The cab driver honked the horn, and we both flinched, Miguel tugging away gently.

"I don't have all night," the cab driver called out the window. "Do you need a ride or... ?"

I went to speak, to hold the driver off a little longer, when my phone rang.

Worse. Timing. Ever.

On instinct, I went to reach for it. It could be something important—Meechie, Denise, or an issue with a contractor.

But the way Miguel's eyes dimmed, visibly pulling into

himself as he pulled away made me stop reaching for my phone. Now was the time to be bold.

Going against everything that was ingrained in me, I let the call go to voicemail. I gripped Miguel's shoulders, forcing him to stay just a little while longer.

"If you come, you come. If you don't, you don't. I won't force you to. Please just think about it."

Miguel eyed me like he was debating what to say, casting glances to the now visibly frustrated driver in the rearview window.

"...Alright. And I'll go to the parade. For *Meech.* Now let me go." He made a point to emphasize for my son and not me.

But it was all I needed. A tiny in, a way to see if what Chris was saying was true. If there was still a chance to salvage the best thing that had happened to me in a very long time.

I let go so he could slip into the cab before the driver took off. And I went back to my car and drove home.

But as I cruised along the road back to Norton Heights, all I could think about was how I could convince Miguel to believe we should give *us* another chance.

CHAPTER 24

MIGUEL

I DIDN'T KNOW HOW I HAD LET DEMETRIUS CONVINCE ME TO GO to the parade. But I plastered on a smile and pulled up at their door like old times, just for Meech's sake.

He bounced out first, eager to see me, and the smile turned real. I jumped out to meet him and bent, scooping him into a hug and twirling him through the air before setting him down.

Even though he was laughing, he shook his head at me with a reproachful look.

"I'm too old for that," he said.

"Oh yeah?"

The door opened again, and Demetrius slipped out, flashing me a shy smile and ending my ability to tease Meech too much.

"Hey," I said, waving.

With Meech here, it didn't feel right to be angry, and I wasn't anymore.

When he walked up to me, bumping our shoulders with a friendly *hello*, all I was filled with was disappointment because things could have been so good between us.

I swallowed and ruffled Meech's short hair, pushing him towards the truck while he grumbled at me.

Demetrius sat next to me. I could feel his eyes on me every couple of seconds, glancing my way, especially when Meech started to go on about his mom, how she was *in town* and they were having the best time. How he wished I could meet her, but she had to do some calls for work this afternoon. Demetrius caught my gaze more than once but didn't say anything.

My knuckles were white by the time we arrived downtown for the parade. The streets were lined with cars already, and crowds had formed along the way, but I knew Gaynor Beach well and parked on a discreet side street.

Meech was beyond excited for the show, and thankfully, I knew it wouldn't disappoint.

There was a reason that Gaynor Beach had such a strong tourism attraction year-round. This town always went out of its way to make the most of every occasion.

While we stood in anticipation, Demetrius leaned closer.

"It's just Meechie and his mom. I don't hang out with them."

I looked at him, confused.

"Why are you telling me this?"

"Because I want you to know. She's here to see Meech, not me. We don't have that kind of love between us anymore."

I frowned, turning back to face the streets.

Either Demetrius was a crueler man than I knew him to be and he wanted to rub in the fact that they weren't together but he still didn't want me, or...

I glanced at him, even more confused.

Nothing had changed. Surely, he wasn't trying to get our failed relationship going again?

Before I could keep wondering, music reached our ears. Sure enough, the marching band started the parade, and they were amazing. People in the crowd started to move, bouncing to the beat, Meech included.

Even Demetrius started to rock side to side, grinning as they passed us.

Again, our gazes met, and his big smile, as usual, did something to me.

I looked away, watching the first float without seeing it at all until Demetrius bumped my shoulder again, trying to get my attention.

"Want something?" he asked, gesturing to the popcorn stand behind us.

I nodded, unconsciously putting an arm around Meech's shoulders as I watched Demetrius walk away.

This was bad. It would be too easy to get roped in again when he was being like this.

I felt like I was under attack and had no clue how to defend myself.

When he returned a few minutes later, the big turkey balloon was being pulled by, floating happily against the blue sky.

He handed me a caramel popcorn and gave one to Meech.

We both took them eagerly.

"Where's yours?" I asked.

"I'm not hungry," he said.

Despite myself, I chuckled.

"You don't need to be hungry for popcorn."

I offered him the bag and he took a couple, popping them in his mouth with an appreciative moan.

We fell silent, watching as kids from the dance school did a routine through the streets.

"We should get you in there for next year!"

Meech shook his head fervently but still watched with rapt attention as they danced past in a fun, upbeat choreo.

I was on the verge of grabbing him and forcing him to

dance with me, imitating their moves. He would probably die from embarrassment, but it would be fun.

Just before I could though, an arm suddenly landed around my shoulders.

I froze, mind not able to catch up to what was happening for a minute.

When I finally looked at Demetrius, he was chewing his bottom lip, gaze fixed to the parade, his cheeks darkened with a deep blush.

This was... unexpected. And I didn't know what to do with it.

Demetrius had never so much as touched me in front of anyone else. He never even stood too close if people were around. He'd been so mortified over someone finding out about us that he had broken it off.

For him to put his arm around me was—for him—a big deal.

And after everything, I didn't know what it meant. Was he subtly coming on to me? Did he want to hook up again? To make amends? Get back together?

Finally, he glanced at me, too nervous to hold my gaze for long, with so much importance in his eyes, that all of my questions were cleared up.

My heart started to beat hard against my chest.

Something like hope, dipped heavily into fear, enveloped my body but I still found myself leaning into him because even just his arm around my shoulders felt good.

We watched the rest of the parade in silence, sharing popcorn, Meech in front of us, oblivious to what was happening behind him.

Even if he looked, he wouldn't notice anything unusual. No one would.

Even in Gaynor Beach, a small town with a popping LGBTQ scene, I doubted that anyone would really think we were together... and we weren't.

This was a nice moment. A reprieve from being alone, I realized. I really didn't think Demetrius wanted anything more than that.

I did though, and I couldn't just jump back in if he wasn't going to be serious. It turned out I cared too much for that.

If he was willing to give me nothing but an arm around the shoulder and the occasional secret hookup, that just wouldn't be enough for me. I wanted all of him.

But in the meantime, I would just enjoy this moment.

Later, when the parade ended and it was time to go home, it didn't hurt as much when it was time to part ways. It was like the friendly half embrace had soothed me a little bit more.

Maybe we could even be friends one day.

I pulled up to their house and Meech, as usual, was the first one out the door, waving at me and thanking me because he was damn polite and had been raised well.

Demetrius lingered, just like he used to.

He reached out, his hand brushed mine.

"Want to come in?" he asked. "I promised Meechie a movie night."

For a moment, I was extremely tempted, ready to unbuckle and dive back into their lives head first. Then I remembered that I'd done this for Meech, not for myself.

I shook my head.

"No, I think it's best to keep some distance, you know."

Demetrius looked genuinely surprised. Then hurt flashed across his eyes and he blinked, looking away.

"Right. About that. I thought maybe—"

"I think you need to figure yourself out," I went on. "How you feel about your ex, your sexuality—"

"I know how I feel," he interrupted. "I'm sorry. I didn't get it. I was overwhelmed. I want you."

That declaration was more than he'd said the entire time we'd been getting to know one another and I was weak and most probably in love, so I couldn't stop myself leaning across the seat and kissing him. Demetrius kissed me back like his life depended on it, his fingers against my jaw, then in my hair, grabbing onto the long locks the way he liked to.

He moaned against my lips.

His hands gripped the front of my shirt desperately and I could *so* go through with this. I could be his boyfriend on the side, always slightly less important than everything else; work, his ex, the opinions of others.

"This is bad," I whispered.

He drew back slightly, watching me, hands still in the hair on the nape of my neck.

"It's not," he insisted. "We can be together. Properly."

I kissed him again. I nearly couldn't pull back the second time.

God, Demetrius was special. The way he made me feel was everything. I would absolutely try for him. I would do anything for him. But only if he returned the sentiment.

"Prove it to me," I finally said, biting my lip to stop from kissing him again.

He was frowning.

"You don't want to be with me unless I prove myself?" he asked, looking confused.

I shook my head, stroking the frown out of his brows.

"Not that. I'm in. Completely," I said. "If you really do want me… It's in your hands."

My voice suddenly shook.

"Just don't make me regret giving you a second chance," I managed in a whisper.

Demetrius stared for a moment longer and then he nodded resolutely.

"I won't," he promised.

Releasing me, he backed up.

He took a deep breath, staring at the dashboard before looking at me with the most determined gaze I'd ever seen.

His hand reached out, squeezing mine.

"You're still coming trick-or-treating, right?" he suddenly asked.

I blinked at the change in topic, but before I could answer, he went on.

"Meech really wants you there."

I nodded numbly and with that, he left me, sitting stunned in the car.

We'd kissed. He'd confessed to wanting to be with me... but it still felt unresolved.

I didn't really know where I stood, but Demetrius was a man of his word. That thought brought a smile to my lips and I lifted a hand, fingers brushing them. They still tingled from his touch.

All I could hope was that he didn't make me regret starting this again. I was powerless when it came to Demetrius.

CHAPTER 25

DEMETRIUS

Trick-or-treating shouldn't be this stressful, I mused as I scratched my chin, standing in front of my bedroom mirror. I pulled on the cheap scarecrow outfit I got at a final sale Halloween pop-up store last minute.

I thought I looked ridiculous, but it reminded me of the plushies me and Miguel had, and showing up in my normal outfit wasn't the right move.

Miguel wanted me to… prove to him that I wanted him. That I was willing to go the extra mile.

That I loved him, hopefully, though saying the big L word might just scare him off. I just got back on speaking and kissing terms, after all. I didn't want to push too hard.

Either way, proving to Miguel that I wanted him meant putting myself out there. Both in my appearance and in the more frightening sense—outing my new and confusing sexuality.

Just a few months ago, even looking at a man sexually never crossed my mind. Now I was going to have to go big and broadcast my attraction to the world.

Well, just a few people in Gaynor Beach, but that was

beside the point. I might as well be broadcasting myself on national television.

I didn't have a label yet for what this feeling was. Why it only seemed to be Miguel after we got closer to each other, just like it used to only to be my ex? I settled on bisexual because it was the easiest to wrap my head around.

But labels weren't nearly as important as what I was really dreading.

Even before Miguel, I was never one for too much PDA. It made me uncomfortable to know that people were watching me or my ex.

But if I wanted Miguel to be *my* man, I had to claim him. Publicly.

I groaned, scratching my head before putting on the matching floppy hat to complete the scarecrow look. Then, still self-conscious about my outfit, I walked downstairs to meet Meechie by the door.

He greeted me with a massive smile, dressed up as a lion with matching face paint. So I guess I didn't look half bad. Or maybe he was happy that he'd get two rounds of candy from going out with Miguel and me tonight and his mom. Probably both.

"Ready?" I asked as I handed him an empty, plastic jack-o-lantern. I had some extra bags in the car just in case he filled up.

"Ready!" he shouted, sprinting to the car, the tail of his lion hoodie bobbing in the air.

He said he didn't "*do*" costumes anymore once he turned eight. Until Denise gifted him that particular hoodie yesterday and painted his face. I was happy I wouldn't be the only one wearing an outfit.

We got in the car and drove down to Gaynor Village, the heart of the city where everyone was going to be.

The ride there was filled with him rattling off names of

people I'd never met and how much we had to hit this one house because this woman gave out full-sized candy bars.

Once we made it, I was happy I had dressed up. I would've stuck out like a sore thumb.

The streets were lined with fake tombstones and spider-webs, creepy music, and gangs of kids hyped on sugar roaming around—the perfect atmosphere for Halloween fun.

Meechie seemed absorbed with filling up his jack-o-lantern. But every once in a while, he would drift back towards me and ask, "Where's Miguel?"

Hell if I knew!

A part of me wondered if I missed the message to pick him up.

I glanced down at my phone. Nothing. Maybe he had backed out.

My heart dropped at the thought that maybe he woke up and decided it wasn't worth the effort of trying once more.

We walked around for quite some time and circled back to where I'd parked to grab the bags. Meechie was content, his pumpkin overflowing with candy. I kept smiling, but my heart was heavier the longer time dragged on.

Until Meechie shot ahead of me, pulling me away from my morbid thoughts.

"Miguel!" he shouted, jumping up and down, waving.

Miguel waved back, keys in his hand, dressed in a cowboy outfit. He was parked not too far from us.

He walked up, and my heart skipped a beat. I was grinning like a fool.

"You made it," I said as he came up beside us.

"Of course. I promised I'd make it for Meech," he said, grinning down at Meechie, who handed him something out of his pumpkin.

Then he looked at me, gaze softening as he popped the piece of candy into his mouth, eyes a gentle shade of green. "And for you."

All I could do was grin back, barely remembering to unlock the door so Meechie could get his extra bags.

When he returned, we started walking on the other side of the street.

Miguel smelled fresh and felt so warm by my side, and the mood felt just right. I reached out and took his hand. My palms were sweaty. But I didn't care.

To my relief, Miguel didn't let go or shoot me a look. Instead, our fingers interlocked, and we passed through the crowds, shoulder to shoulder, hand in hand, as Meechie raced ahead of us in my line of sight but just out of reach.

He hadn't noticed, I didn't think.

I kept trying to find the perfect time to do it. But I kept getting caught up in my thoughts, second-guessing.

As we reached the fourth house on this side of the block, Meechie hopped up the stairs to get his treat, and Miguel leaned into me and whispered in my ear.

"You know, a little hand-holding isn't going to make me forgive you, Demetrius. Not just yet."

Was he teasing me or telling the truth? I couldn't tell by the look on his face, though he was smiling.

Maybe there wasn't a perfect time to admit it, but I went for it, anyway. It was now or never. The least Miguel deserved.

"I know. And I've been meaning to say this from the start. I... I-I want us to date, Miguel. Openly. I want us to be together because I think... Err... Well, I think I... Uh..."

Damn my shaking hands. Like I was in high school or something. I reached up to cup Miguel's face and did the only thing I could think to do to "prove it." By kissing him where everyone could see us, the kids from Meechie's school, their parents, hell, maybe even that female art teacher he kept talking about recently, too.

His lips were sweet, slightly sticky from whatever Meechie had given him. I usually hated anything too sweet, but Miguel tasted just right, as he always did. But I was over-eager, and our hats bumped against each other, teeth colliding with lips, and I couldn't help but laugh as I pulled away from the botched kiss.

I didn't know what to expect when I opened my eyes. I looked at Miguel, my hand shaking slightly, still holding his. I didn't dare look around, forcing myself not to care what other people thought of me for once. I was relieved to find only reassurance in his soft, hazel eyes as they shifted in color.

We stood like that for God knew how long, hand in hand, grinning, a little shy.

"Ummmm...."

Oh, shit.

I turned to see Meechie looking at our hands with confusion from the steps as he walked down. Then he looked up at me with the same look and a timid smile.

I didn't have it in me to explain everything to him right then and there. But I would, when the time was right. Or maybe the time would never be right, and I should just say something.

"Ready for more trick-or-treating?" Miguel broke the silence, practically dragging me forward.

Meech kept staring at our interlocked hands before nodding enthusiastically. Of course, we'd have to talk about what Miguel meant to me at some point.

I was happy not to have that conversation right now, still savoring the taste of Miguel's lips, and glad that I found the courage to go after what I wanted.

I didn't know where this new relationship was going to take me.

But we would find our way together.

One step at a time.

CHAPTER 26

MIGUEL

DEMETRIUS KISSING ME IN FRONT OF ALL THOSE PEOPLE MEANT A lot, but the fact that he wasn't pretending in front of Meech meant more.

I knew how much he adored his son; he was his whole world, and the two of them were quickly becoming mine.

For Meech to know showed me how serious Demetrius was about us. Especially since he looked like a nervous wreck when he did it.

I couldn't help feeling a little bit guilty about it. A month ago, Demetrius hadn't even known he was interested in men, and now he was officially out of the closet, openly dating one.

And just like the first time I'd had him in my bed, I felt deeply honored and grateful. I just wanted to *kiss* him. So I did.

It was a quick peck; I knew we were on a busy street and wasn't going to make a scene with Meech there. Just being able to press our lips together when I felt like it made my heart sing and when I pulled back, Demetrius was biting back that smile that always undid me. I couldn't take my eyes off of him, even in the silly costume, hat now askew because I'd bumped it with my own.

Meech noticed. I saw him pretending not to see. He was classy though, just like his dad and he waited until we were walking back to the car, bags full of candy to finally say something.

"What's happening?" he asked.

I glanced at Demetrius, leaving it to him to explain unless he needed me to help. He didn't though, he just stopped, letting me go and turning to face Meech.

"Miguel and I... we really care for each other. In a romantic way."

We waited while Meech seemed to process this. My heart was in my throat. I could only imagine what Demetrius was experiencing.

"Are you two in love?" he asked finally.

Demetrius didn't even hesitate.

"Yes," he said and then looked at me with his eyes wide. "I mean, I am—"

"I am too," I said firmly, and he visibly sank with relief, tearing his gaze away to face his son again.

Again, Meech thought it over, looking between us before ultimately shrugging.

"I guess that's good then," he said.

He started to walk again, like that was that, and I found myself laughing. The simplicity of the way children dealt with these things was the best. They had to be taught hate, and Demetrius and Denise had clearly been better than that.

Demetrius looked like a literal weight had been lifted. He trailed after us, shaking his head until we reached his car.

"Need a lift?" he asked, reaching out to catch my hand again. Then, in a lower voice, he added, "I'm dropping Meech off with Denise. They're going to hit the shops. Then he's staying at her hotel for the night..."

I glanced into the car, making sure Meech couldn't see this time when I leaned in and pressed our lips together. He might have been cool with it, but that didn't mean he needed to see his dad smooching his boyfriend constantly.

"I drove here," I said.

"We can pick up your car in the morning," he whispered, and really, how could I keep arguing?

I practically jumped into the back. Meech had taken the passenger seat. As usual, the banter and chatter was easy between the three of us.

Meech was buzzing, possibly because he'd already eaten four chocolate bars that I had counted. When we got downtown, Denise was waiting at the corner nearest to Nice Buns. Meech bounded out, holding his jack-o-lantern full of candy and the extra two bags he'd filled up in the air, shouting to her across the street.

She looked just like her picture, beautiful and elegant. When Meech reached her, she stooped to hug him, laughing.

She waved at the car, then pointed at the nearest shop and off they went.

It didn't seem like she had seen me in the back but if she had, she didn't make it obvious.

There was an ease between us when we got back to his place. He pulled me inside eagerly and kissed me hungrily, but also insisted on popping popcorn and filling a bowl with the left over Halloween candy as well.

We crashed on the couch, half in each other's arms, watching random Halloween episodes of old shows on TV that we grew up watching. There was something about Halloween, the costumes and sour candies and the thrill of trying to scare people that was so exciting.

Demetrius was still in his scarecrow outfit, sprawled out on the couch, his hat laying on the coffee table next to mine.

We looked ridiculous and silly and happy.

He was ignoring me, watching the TV with a lollipop in his mouth when I couldn't stop myself from leaning over, pulling it free from his lips and taking a lick.

He watched me, gaze instantly darkening.

Without hesitation, he slid his hand into the hair at my nape and pulled me in for a kiss, tongue delving between my lips.

He was cherry flavored and delicious, sending a thrill of electricity through my body.

When he pushed me down flat against the cushions, I went easily, only breaking away to say, "I thought the couch was a no-no."

He grinned.

"I'm trying new things. So far, it seems to be working for me."

"Speaking of which..." I let my words trail off. He was in between my thighs, so I wrapped my legs around his waist, lifting to grind against his cock. "I think we got interrupted last time we were going to try something new."

He let out a shuddering breath and bent down, pressing me down with another deep kiss that made my head reel.

When he pulled back and started unbuttoning the front of my shirt, it took me a minute to realize I should help.

I was hard and eager, my entire body hot with want. I'd give him anything, and I liked going top or bottom anyway, but he acted like I was doing him a favor, taking his time sucking my cock when he got there, taking it deep until I was twisting up into his mouth, close to the edge, and then pulling away, lowering his lips to my balls and then behind, licking the sensitive skin there before settling at my hole.

He was meticulous, taking his time on the outside, waiting until my body started to react, hole tightening and flexing before he pressed his tongue deeper.

I was shuddering and leaking pre-cum by the time he started with his fingers, pressing them inside me almost reverently, watching my face for every reaction, and then gripping me around the cock to stop me from twitching or wiggling too much.

"I can't take much more," I groaned, and he finally pulled his fingers out.

He pulled his shirt over his head, tossed it, and then shoved his pants down, exposing his hard cock. It was wet too, a drop glistening on the tip which he used to rub against my entrance before using saliva to slick the rest of his length.

When he pushed forward, I instinctively forced my muscles to relax. There was a slight resistance and then, suddenly, he slid inside, stretching me around him.

We both moaned, and he stilled, his hips tight against my ass.

It had been a while, but he'd loosened me up enough that the stretch just felt good. My eyes rolled when he started to move and my head fell back. A moan tore from my throat with each thrust, sparks of pleasure making my cock jerk sporadically, pre-cum practically pouring.

When Demetrius' rhythm changed, growing shorter, jerkier as he tried to hold on, I reached down, clamping my cock in my fist and pulling.

He gasped, watching me, and then, his rhythm really faltered, hips shaking and he slammed into me, coming. The silky heat of his come filling me sent me over the edge, and I clamped down on his cock, milking the last drops as I came, moaning his name and cursing.

"Oh fuck," he gasped, dropping his forehead onto my shoulder as he fought for air. "That was incredible."

I moaned in agreement and wiggled my hips, relishing the wet feeling of him still inside me.

He gasped, pressed deeper for a second, and then gently pulled free.

His head ended up on my shoulder, arms around me as he relaxed on top of me, showing no signs of going anywhere.

Next to us, the TV still played and I wrapped my arms around him, feeling sated and happy.

I couldn't believe how much I'd grown to care about this

person in my arms. Without exaggerating, it felt like I had been waiting for him all this time.

The fact that we'd nearly let it end was crazy to me now.

"I honestly don't know what I would have done if we didn't get back together," I mused, gently stroking his back. "You mean more to me than someone I've known for less than two months has any right to."

I felt him smile and he lifted his head, resting his chin on my chest so we could look at each other.

"I can only imagine what it'll feel like in another couple months."

"I know exactly what it'll feel like: perfection."

He chuckled, but his gaze was warm.

"I meant what I said to Meech," he whispered. "I love you."

I closed the distance between us, kissing him gently before replying.

"I love you too."

It was crazy, maybe even foolish, but it didn't feel that way. It felt warm and secure and stable. It felt like we were made to lean on each other. Like we were meant to love each other.

That was what I was going with anyway.

Demetrius was the one I'd been looking for; for adventures, love, and raising a family. For so many years, I'd sought more in life, always looking for the next thing. Until settling here and realizing what really mattered.

Demetrius fulfilled my every desire, and together, I knew, our adventure was just starting.

EPILOGUE

DEMETRIUS

One Year Later

LOVE WAS IN THE AIR. THAT AND THE SMELL OF GLAZED HAM, stuffed turkey, and steamy collard greens.

A year had come and gone in a flash, filled with more adventures and tender moments in Gaynor Beach with Miguel. I didn't expect things to fall into place so perfectly once I confessed, and now I wished I could go back and just say it back on that pier before everything went south.

I smiled to myself, arranging silverware on the dinner table. We had too many guests at my house for all of us to sit down for a meal.

We were definitely going to have to buy a bigger house if each Thanksgiving was going to look like this, filled with kids running around and adults squished into corners. And that didn't include my parents or more of our friends. And while he didn't celebrate it as much as he did Christmas, I knew Hiroshi was desperate to show off his grandbabies and arrange playdates whenever he could.

So, maybe a move was in our near future.

Maybe.

Miguel hadn't officially moved in yet, though he might as well have. His toothbrush, changes of clothing, and all sorts of little pieces of him were all around our home. His lease would be up soon. And then, maybe…

I was getting ahead of myself again. Relaxing and going with the flow was proving to be more worthwhile each day. I didn't want to jinx what was shaping up to be a perfect day by getting too in my head again.

"Slow down," I said as Meech—who now insisted I called him Meech, not Meechie because he was too old for that—zoomed past me.

He was followed by a boy his age named Perry, both of them laughing loudly, probably up to no good as they raced up the stairs.

Before I could tell them to come back down, someone asked, "Is dinner almost ready?"

I looked to the couch. Dan and his oldest daughter, Lexi, were watching the Giants play the Austin Troopers, a new NFL franchise, on the brand new flatscreen. I guess it would be better to say he was watching football and Lexi was busy playing on her tablet watching a local children's entertainer she enjoyed. I thought his name was either Erick or Ethan Mack. I couldn't remember exactly. Hiroshi had told me about him and how he was building a home library for his grandson starting with his books. A little overzealous since they couldn't hold their heads up, let alone enjoy being read a book. But it was cute, nonetheless.

Dan turned to me with a huge smile, bouncing his one-year-old on his knee, who was gurgling loudly.

"Dinner?" he asked again, his smile growing.

"About twenty, no fifteen more minutes," his wife responded before I could, helping me out by grabbing plates to finish setting the table.

Having Dan and his family over for Thanksgiving was Miguel's idea. I was a little nervous at first since I only knew Dan as the former PM, not as a close friend. But it had all worked out for the best. And made things more lively, that was for sure.

"Tri, can you get the cornbread and the cups?" Denise asked, balancing a piping hot sweet potato pie in her gloved hands.

I did, so happy that, somehow, we'd worked things out. I really was worried that things wouldn't work out for a second there. Denise did get a little distant after the whole phone fiasco, remaining civil, but obviously a little weirded out. It wasn't like she was best friends with Miguel or something ridiculous like that.

But she came and wasn't just civil, putting on a show. She was genuinely having a good time. Happy to be around us and help out in the kitchen, which was a plus. I was never a fantastic cook, so I wanted this year's dinner to be perfect. Last year's was store bought.

This was more than I could've ever asked for since the most awkward moment of my life.

And the more I looked at her, I could see Denise was glowing. A little too much, actually. I had a sneaking suspicion that there was something more to it than just starting a new job and being closer to Meech.

But she'd tell me, when the time was right, when we were ready to let the last tendrils of awkwardness disappear as we fully stepped into co-parents, and maybe someday soon, friends again.

"Meech! Perry? Come down here and eat."

I could hear something being knocked over upstairs. They'd been out of sight, out of mind for too long.

I frowned, hearing them murmur. I hoped something didn't get broken.

When they didn't immediately come running down the stairs, I went to go after them. But then two large arms wrapped around my waist and stopped me in my tracks.

"Miguel?"

"Mmmm. Just let them play and come sit down."

I wondered when he got back from the store. Somehow we'd forgotten to get cranberry juice, and it wouldn't be Thanksgiving without cranberry juice. At least not for me.

"But they need to come down and eat. Or at least stop breaking shit," I murmured back, giving him a quick peck on the cheek.

He was still a little too lovey-dovey for my liking. But we were home, and he was warm and sweet and his lips pressed discreetly against my neck felt so good.

Open, honest, as embarrassing as it was. I preferred it now rather than sneaking around after dark.

As I went to pull away, two little heads poked through the banister of the staircase. I couldn't help but laugh at their faces, desperately trying to hide whatever secret they were trying to hide.

They didn't hide it for long.

Meech, in his usual unfiltered way, blurted out, "Are you guys getting married?"

I froze mid-turn, trying to unravel myself from Miguel's arms. My eyes shot open, as well as my finger to my lips.

"What!" I said, a little too loudly.

I heard Dan clear his throat, his wife giggle, and even his daughter snort. I was going to pass out like this was some sort of soap opera.

To my dismay, Meech produced a golden wedding band, his new friend holding up the other.

"We didn't mean to, but we sorta found these and I figured it was yours and Miguel's."

Damn it.

They must have knocked over the box I was hiding in the upstairs closet. Probably saw the ring box while they tried to hide what they'd done.

But I didn't care about all that, or why they were in the closet in the first place.

"So... are you?" Meech followed up, eyes twinkling.

"Meech!" Denise hissed, shaking her head hard, locs flying through the air. "What did I tell you about getting in grown folks' business!"

It was too late. The rings, and my maybe-soon-I-hadn't-decided proposal, were out of the box.

My lips flopped like a fish as I turned to face Miguel. There wasn't anything I could say with the evidence dangling from the banister right in front of us. But this was the exact opposite of how I wanted my proposal to go.

Waiting, as always, for that perfect moment. Something more romantic. At the very least not with the sound of football in the background and the smell of yams in the air.

Maybe at the pier, where I first realized my feelings and we had our first not-really date. Anything other than this.

But, as always, Miguel took things in stride. His eyes were so warm, his mouth fighting to hold back a smile. I knew he wanted to kiss me silly, but I could also see him struggle, knowing my heart really would give out if he did.

So he settled on pulling me into a fierce hug, and it was all the confirmation I needed. Or, more accurately, could take. I didn't think my heart was going to hold up from Meech unintentionally outing me anymore.

But then, my pounding heart settled, beating at a slow and steady pace. And I was overcome with emotion, burying my face into Miguel's shoulder.

All I ever wanted was right here, in my arms, surrounding me too, making this house a home.

I was no longer running from my past. Far from it, I was

facing reality head on, rebuilding relationships, and forging new ones. And each day building a better future with the man of my dreams.

———

The End

NEXT IN THE GAYNOR BEACH SERIES

LEO BY MEREDITH SPIES

The funeral business is burying me. Entrusted with Morris Funeral Home and Crematorium, the company that has been in my family for four generations, I fear it's going to go belly up under the growing pile of bills. But the troubles haunting me don't end there. My son's teachers don't seem to understand how to work with a kid like Eddie, leaving me zero time for myself.

Then there's Ambrose Jennings. The quirky baker is catering Delia Dennis' funeral and I can't seem to get him out of my head.

The last thing I need right now is any kind of romantic complications in my life. Still, Ambrose is boisterous fun and chaos wrapped up in a sexy, tempting package. Maybe one little taste of the baker's goods wouldn't be the end of the world..?

When Ambrose gives me a sample of the sweet treats he has on offer, both of us ache for this to become more than a taste test. I don't know if it's enough to let go of my reservations, or if circumstances close the coffin in their chances for any future together.

https://books2read.com/leosingledadsofgaynorbeach

ALSO SET IN GAYNOR BEACH

Single Dads of Gaynor Beach Series

Finn by Jessie G

Wynn by Amelia Hayden

Hugh by Gabbi Grey

Anderson by Foxy Valentine

Alec by Kaje Harper

Demetrius by SA Sway & Skyler Drake

Leo by Meredith Spies

Anthony by Gabbi Grey

Hiroshi by Skyler Drake

Jaime by SA Sway

Nate by Amelia Hayden

Tress by Michele Shriver

Eden by Leona Windwalker

Xavier by Gabbi Grey

Mattie by Elouise East

Lucien by Alice La Roux

———

Friends of Gaynor Beach Animal Rescue

Love Furever by Gabbi Grey

Impurrfections by Kate Harper

Iguana You to Want Me by Meredith Spies

Husky Love by Gabbi Grey

Ruff Start by Roan Rosser

Yorkie to My Heart by Gabbi Grey

A Furry Thing Called Love by Abrianna Denae

AUTHOR NOTE

Thank you for reading *Demetrius!* We think this story can definitely be classified as "sweet-with-heat," and it was really fun to try and stuff as many fall/autumn events into their love story. Special shout out to our wonderful editor, Ashley, and our secret co-co-writer who works in construction and helped us make things a little more plausible. It was a blast co-writing this book, and both SA and Skyler will be back in Gaynor Beach soon! We really hope you consider leaving a review as it would really help out the book. And check out all the other books in the series, including our next two: *Hiroshi*, coming out in January 2023, and *Jamie*, debuting March 2023. Thank you!

– SA Sway & Skyler Drake

MORE BY SA SWAY

CONTEMPORARY:

The Shooting Star Series

Inevitable

Unattainable

Unloveable

Intolerable

Single Dads of Gaynor Beach Series

Demetrius

Jaime

FANTASY:

The Mismatched Princes Series

The Oaf's Prince

The Elf's Prince

SCIENCE FICTION:

The Alien's Omega Series

The Alien's Kidnapped Omega

The Alien's Stolen Omega

www.siennasway.com

MORE BY SKYLER DRAKE

Achillean Romance

Standalones

The Desert Prince's Jewel

Imprisoned by the Wizard

Tethered Souls Trilogy

Tethered Souls

Tethered Desire

Tethered Throne

Delta Rangers Series

Delta Moon

Delta Star

Delta Rangers

Delta Sun

ABOUT THE AUTHORS

SA Sway is the contemporary pen name of Sienna Sway. She's a Canadian, a mother, and an author who writes M/M romance of all genres. She is a romantic at heart and a lover of happy endings.

Social Media:
Twitter: @siennasway
Goodreads: https://www.goodreads.com/siennasway
BookBub: https://bookbub.com/profile/2515736759
TikTok: https://www.tiktok.com/@siennaswayauthor
Instagram: https://www.instagram.com/siennasway/
Twitter: https://twitter.com/siennasway

————

SKYLER DRAKE is an author of spicy and diverse LGBTQ+ contemporary, sci-fi, and fantasy romances.

Newsletter: https://crownebooks.com/newsletter

Social Media:
https://www.facebook.com/crownebooks
https://www.instagram.com/crownebooks
https://www.tiktok.com/@crownebooks
https://www.youtube.com/@crownebooks
https://www.threads.com/@crownebooks
https://www.goodreads.com/crownebooks

www.ingramcontent.com/pod-product-compliance
Lightning Source LLC
Chambersburg PA
CBHW022145240626
47153CB00007B/2514